Hostage
– on the –
Nighthawk

Trailblazer Books

*Hero Tales: A Family Treasury of True Stories
From the Lives of Christian Heroes* (Volumes I, II, III, & IV)

*Curriculum guide available.

Written by Julia Pferdehirt with Dave & Neta Jackson.

Hostage
– on the –
Nighthawk

Dave & Neta Jackson

Story illustrations by
Anne Gavitt

BETHANY HOUSE PUBLISHERS
MINNEAPOLIS, MINNESOTA 55438

Published by Bethany House Publishers
A Ministry of Bethany Fellowship International
11400 Hampshire Avenue South
Minneapolis, Minnesota 55438
www.bethanyhouse.com

Printed in the United States of America by
Bethany Press International, Minneapolis, Minnesota 55438

Library of Congress Cataloging-in-Publication Data

Jackson, Dave.
    Hostage on the Nighthawk : Governor William Penn / Dave & Neta Jackson.
        p.   cm. — (Trailblazer books)
    SUMMARY: While held hostage on a pirate ship in 1700, thirteen-year-old Theo escapes with his sister and enlists the help of William Penn to rescue their mother.

ISBN 0–7642–2265–1 (pbk.)
    [1. Hostages—Fiction. 2. Pirates—Fiction. 3. Escapes—Fiction. 4. Rescues—Fiction. 5. Penn, William, 1644?–1718—Fiction.] I. Jackson, Neta. II. Title.
PZ7.J132418   Ho   2000
[Fic]—dc21   99–050774

The depiction of William Penn is factual. Penn's trusted associate, Thomas Story, was a Quaker and a lawyer, who preceded him to Pennsylvania by one year to prepare for Penn's return to the colony. Story, however, was only in his late twenties at this time and did not have a wife, Abigail, or the two children we call Theodore and Nicole. The events directly pertaining to them, the *Loyal Tradesman*, the *Nighthawk*, and the *Phoenix* are fictional. Though Tammany is an authentic Indian name, he, too, is fictional.

Captain Kidd is another matter. After several years at sea, he had hoped to return to his home in New York to enjoy his newly gotten wealth as a privateer. But upon arriving in the West Indies and discovering that he was wanted for piracy, he sailed north very cautiously. He stopped in Delaware Bay for two days, where he transferred some of his men, bales of goods, and various chests into an unnamed ship. After his arrest on July 6, 1699, in Boston, he claimed that, if allowed, he could retrieve £70,000 in treasure. Though there are numerous legends of Captain Kidd's treasure being buried in the area, there is no further record of the ship we call the *Nighthawk* and no report of Kidd's pirates attacking any ships after his arrest. However, Robert Quary, William Penn's customs collector, did capture two of Kidd's men in the vicinity of Delaware Bay, and William Penn himself put Captain Kidd's doctor in prison.

Interestingly, years later a heavy copper-bound chest was briefly recovered from the Delaware River just below Philadelphia, but it was immediately lost.

Find us on the Web at . . .

trailblazerbooks.com

- Meet the authors.

- Read the first chapter of each book—
  with the pictures.

- Track the Trailblazers around the world
  on a map.

- Use the historical timeline to find out
  what other important events were happening in the world at the time of each
  Trailblazer story.

- Discover how the authors research their
  books and link to some of the same
  sources they used where
  you can learn more
  about these heroes.

- Write to the authors.

- Explore frequently asked
  questions about writing
  and Trailblazer books.

Just point your browser to http://www.trailblazerbooks.com

CONTENTS

DAVE AND NETA JACKSON are a full-time husband/wife writing team who have authored and coauthored many books on marriage and family, the church, relationships, and other subjects. Their books for children include the TRAILBLAZER series and *Hero Tales,* volumes I, II, and III. The Jacksons have two married children, Julian and Rachel, and make their home in Evanston, Illinois.

Chapter 1

The Cannon Blast

WOULD SHE NEVER HUSH? Theodore Story sighed and hunched his shoulders against the brisk December wind. Everyone was tired of waiting. And it was cold just standing on the dock. But couldn't his little sister understand that pestering every five minutes with "Is he coming now?" would not make the governor appear any sooner?

Sailing up the Delaware River on its way to Philadelphia, the governor's ship, *Canterbury,* had stopped for the night at the town of Chester. But this morning, with December ice still crackling in the ship's rigging, Governor William Penn had remained on board. Surely with such a large crowd waiting to salute him, he would come ashore soon.

Theo's father, Thomas Story, worked as an aide for Governor Penn, a Quaker, and had brought his family down from Philadelphia to meet him. It was their first outing as a family since the loss of their three-year-old, Jessica, to yellow fever just a month ago, and Theo's mother was trying hard to be cheerful. They'd been in Pennsylvania only a year when the yellow fever epidemic struck. The Story family had come ahead to help prepare for the governor's return from England, where he had been for fifteen long years. Now the governor had finally arrived, so Thomas Story, his wife, Abigail, and Theo and Nicole stood waiting on the river dock along with a festive crowd of other citizens.

Again Theo looked out at the silent ship. He couldn't see anyone on deck. Restless, the lanky thirteen-year-old turned and pushed through the crowd, looking for his friend Bernie Bevan. Bernie had also come down from Philadelphia to greet the governor. Everyone thought it would be such a good time, but so far, all they had done was wait. Theo had last seen freckle-faced Bernie heading up the trail toward the top of the bluff overlooking the river with a skinny kid named Charles, a boy he'd met here in Chester. Bernie was smart—when you're from out of town and don't know what to do, find someone local to show you some fun.

The trail was steep, and the exercise warmed Theo's blood. His breath came out in little steam puffs as he neared the top of the bluff. He loosened the wool scarf around his neck and stepped through some brush into an open area.

"Hey, Theo, look at this!" called a gleeful voice. "We're *really* gonna welcome the governor!"

Redheaded Bernie stood beside an old rusty cannon that was pointed toward the river, while Chester worked with a ramrod pushing something down its barrel.

Theo waved an arm at the half circle of huge stone blocks evenly spaced along the edge of the bluff. "What's this, the top of a castle?" He could now see there were actually two cannons poking out between the stones. A small wooden powder keg sat on the ground between them.

Charles stood up, his ankles hanging out below the bottom of his pant legs. "It's what's left of the old Dutch fort that used to guard the river."

Noting the direction the cannon was pointed, Theo rushed forward to the edge and looked. "You're not going to fire on the governor's ship, are you?"

"Yeah! We're gonna blow him out of the water the moment he steps into his little boat to be rowed ashore," laughed Bernie. Charles joined in, and together they roared with nervous excitement.

Theo looked over the edge to the ship sitting at anchor in the river. The cannon *did* seem to be pointed right at it. "You can't do that!" he sputtered.

Charles raised both arms shoulder high as though he were welcoming the whole world. With a wide-eyed, silly grin, he said, "Why not?"

"Because . . ." Theo looked from one boy to the

other. This couldn't be happening.

Bernie slapped him on the shoulder. "Hey, you're too gullible, Story. Why would we want to shoot at the governor? We're just going to give him a royal salute—just a big boom. You don't see any cannonballs sitting around here, do you?"

"You rats," Theo said and socked Bernie in the chest as he turned and walked away. He felt like a fool, falling for their story. Of course they wouldn't shoot the governor! Even though William Penn had been away for a long time, everyone loved him. Today was the first day of December 1699, and he was returning just in time to take the colony into the new century.

"Come on, Theo," called Bernie. "Be a sport. Here, you can help us fire it." But Theo continued to walk toward the trail that would take him back down the hill.

"Hey, you aren't going to tell on us, are you?" asked Charles.

Theo stopped and turned. Why were they worried that he might tell? He walked back toward the boys, studying their faces. "What's there to tell? As soon as you fire that thing, everybody is going to know what you did."

Bernie and Charles glanced at each other as though trying to decide whether to let Theo in on their secret. "Uh . . . well," said Bernie, grinning, "when Charles asked if we could shoot off a cannon, the mayor said no. 'Absolutely not!' " he mimicked. " 'Nobody is s'posed to mess with those cannons.' "

"He told you—! So why are you doing it?"

Charles shrugged. "The mayor's an old goat. Doesn't want anyone to have fun. But you wait and see; when all those people hear *our* salute, they'll cheer. Then the mayor will probably tell them he asked us to fire it."

Theo looked from Charles to Bernie. He had heard that the mayor of Chester was a rather stiff-laced old man and that things in this little town were not nearly so free as in Philadelphia just a few miles up the river. But if the mayor specifically told Charles *not* to fire the cannon . . . "You guys go ahead and have a good time. Think I'll go back down. My folks will be wondering where I am before long, and you wouldn't want my father coming up here."

"Do as you please." Bernie shrugged and turned back to the cannon.

"Just don't tell anyone what we're doing up here," Charles warned. "We want it to be a surprise!"

Theo arrived back at the dock just as people started clapping and cheering. Making his way through the crowd to where his parents and sister stood, he could see that Governor Penn, his wife and daughter, and another young man were finally in the longboat.

"Look, Theo!" said Nicole, dancing up and down on her toes, her brown curls bouncing. "He's coming! And Mrs. Penn and Latitia are with him, too. Do you think she'll remember me?"

Theo rolled his eyes. Penn's daughter by his first wife, practically a grown woman, had always fussed over Nicole and little Jessica. Theo's heart gave a sudden lurch at the thought of his baby sister, dead now. He shook his head and squinted toward the anchored ship.

Slowly some sailors pushed the boat away from the ship and began to row toward shore. Both women and the young man were seated, but the genteel governor remained standing beside the ship's officer who held the tiller. His curly hair, whitened more by powder than by his fifty-five years, fell gently to his shoulders and outlined his full oval face. Even from that distance, Theo noted the governor's calm gaze as he waved to the people on the dock.

As the boat moved smoothly through the gray, placid water, Theo looked back at the top of the bluff where the old cannons poked out between the huge stones. He could see Bernie and Charles moving around. Had they lost their courage? Were they reconsidering their plan? And then Theo saw Bernie's curly head as he looked over the edge. He had a smoking puck in his hand. Now was the time. Would he do it?

Bernie disappeared, and a moment later a huge cloud of white smoke billowed from the cannon followed by a thunderous boom that rocked the riverfront. A few women screamed, but everyone turned to look up at the old fort. As the smoke drifted away, the two boys climbed to the top of the stones on either side of the cannon and waved their arms in triumph.

The crowd cheered, and then, as though someone pulled a string to turn their heads, everyone's attention shifted to see how the governor would respond. But he was alternately clapping and waving to the boys.

Just as Charles had predicted, the mayor's voice called out from the riverside, "Well done, lads! Very well done!" as though he had ordered the cannon shot.

It was a great demonstration, and Theo hadn't been part of it. He hung his head and started to kick at a loose board in the dock when his father's sudden movement almost knocked him over. "Oh *no!*" Thomas Story gasped.

Theo looked up at the cliff where his father was staring, openmouthed. Bernie was pushing another powder charge down the barrel of the cannon with the ram. He pushed it deeper.

"No, No, NO!" yelled Mr. Story. "It's still hot! The powder will blow!"

Again white smoke billowed, but with the boom that followed, two objects flew out of the smoke, tumbling end over end and falling into the bushes at the bottom of the cliff. Theo jerked in horror. One was Bernie . . . the other looked like his arm!

Shock froze the crowd until a woman screamed. Then mothers hugged their small children into their skirts and men started running for the base of the cliff.

"Is there a doctor here?" Theo's father yelled. "Theo, go find Dr. Simpson."

Theo hesitated. He wanted to go to Bernie! Was he alive? Had that really been his arm? What if he was bleeding to death!

"I be a doctor." A scruffy man in a three-cornered hat stepped forward, waving his hand toward Mr. Story, but Theo's father was already running up the hill. The man looked around at the frowning people who were staring at him. "Just call me Dr. Patch." He grinned and pointed to the patch over his right eye. "I been a ship's doctor for many a year and have seen this kind of injury all too often." He started off toward Bernie, and Theo hurried after him, noticing that the man with the patch had a limp in his left leg.

Bernie's fall down the cliff had been broken by some tough bushes, on which he now lay like a rag doll. His eyes were closed, his face white. Blood soaked the right side of his wool coat. Theo hardly recognized him.

"I'm a doctor," the strange man said again. "Help me get the boy down off this bush. Put him on the ground with his head uphill."

Mr. Story and a couple other men helped.

"Easy, now," growled Dr. Patch. "The lad could 'ave broken bones, and we don't want to make matters worse."

Dr. Patch worked quickly to stop the bleeding from Bernie's shoulder. He sure looked like he knew what he was doing.

Theo couldn't pull his eyes away from the horror of his friend's missing arm until the little circle of onlookers parted to let the mayor and William Penn through. The governor's kind face was etched with concern.

"I *told* them not to fire that cannon!" said the

hawk-faced mayor, wringing his hands. "I warned those boys, but children just don't listen to their elders anymore. I declare, Governor, I just don't know what's going to become of this world in the next century."

But no one was paying any attention to what the mayor said, least of all Theo. His friend was dying on the ground right in front of him. He felt so helpless. What could he do? What could he do? He looked around. There had to be something! If only he could turn back the clock. He'd known what the boys were going to do. He should have stopped them. But how? They wouldn't have listened to him. Maybe he should have told his father . . . but you don't just tell on your friends. Still . . . he had known, and he hadn't told, and now Bernie was going to die.

Minutes dragged. Finally Dr. Patch stood up and shook his head. He looked at Governor Penn. "Don't know if the lad'll be makin' it. He needs ongoing medical care—something I can't give him." Noticing the question on the governor's face, he added, "Seein' as how I'll be back at sea a'fore the mornin'."

Theo stared hard at Bernie. His friend looked as close to dead as anyone Theo had ever seen. But no, there was a slight movement in his chest. He was still breathing, and the doctor said he needed *ongoing* medical attention. "He's going to make it, isn't he, Doc?"

The doctor raised the eyebrow over his patch and squinted at Theo out of his other eye. "Him that knows is keepin' mum, son. But frankly, I fear he's destined for Davy Jones's locker . . . if he were at sea, that is."

The words stabbed Theo. *Why* hadn't he told someone? His mind was spinning so fast he hardly heard the governor say, "I take it, sir, that you are a ship's doctor?"

"Oh, that I be, that I be," said Dr. Patch as he raised his three-pointed hat with one hand and wiped his brow with the back of his other hand, leaving a brown streak of Bernie's blood across his forehead. "I've breathed the salt air for so many years that my nose gets all stuffed up when I come ashore, and I can't seem to walk a straight line if there's no deck rolling under me feet. So I never stay ashore for long."

"Yes," said William Penn, stroking his chin and frowning as he looked the doctor up and down. "I can imagine you might have some difficulty walking . . . the straight and narrow, that is. And what, may I ask, is the name of your ship?"

But instead of answering, Dr. Patch knelt down beside Bernie and felt his forehead. "You say there be a doctor in town?"

"Dr. Simpson," said one of the Chester citizens. "We've sent to fetch him."

The governor spoke up. "We're grateful for your efforts on behalf of this poor young man, uh, doctor. If you'll name the price . . ."

Dr. Patch stood up with a glint in his eye. "Well, that would be . . . twenty guineas. Twenty guineas for saving the lad's life."

Governor Penn pursed his lips. But he said, "I'll have your fee sent to your ship tonight before you sail in the morning."

"Oh, now, Governor, I wouldn't want an important man like yourself to have to come all the way to me ship. Whatever is convenient now will be payment enough. I'm just happy to serve a mate in need."

The governor scowled as he felt in the pocket of his waistcoat and pulled out several coins that he handed to the man.

"Thank you kindly," said the doctor as he took the coins, biting on one to make sure they were not made of lead. Then his face reddened. "Forgive me, Your Honor. It's just that these days you never know. Good day!" He doffed his three-cornered hat and turned to leave. The people in the circle around Bernie parted to let him pass.

"What a rude man," Theo's father muttered.

The governor continued to look after the doctor as he limped away. "Hmm. I wonder what ship he does sail on?" He turned to Theo's father thoughtfully. "Story, have you continued having as much trouble with pirates as you wrote in your letter last spring?"

"Well, yes. But we hope it's over. You heard that Captain Kidd was captured, didn't you?"

"Yes, yes, I did," the governor mused. "But I also heard that he almost escaped!"

Chapter 2

The Holy Experiment

ONCE DR. SIMPSON ARRIVED and carried Bernie away in his carriage, the crowd attempted to regain a joyful spirit in welcoming the governor. A few men made speeches, and people clapped half-heartedly, but Theo sat on a low piling at the end of the dock with his head in his hands. He felt sick over what he had seen and thought he might lose his breakfast into the river at any moment.

Finally the ceremonies were over. "Theo," his father said, "come on. It's time to go. We can't do anything more for Bernie now."

Reluctantly Theo joined his parents and Governor Penn's party, and together they all got in the ship's longboat. As the sailors rowed them out to the *Canterbury*,

Theo studied the newcomers. Both women looked nearly the same age, but he knew the quieter one was Penn's new wife, Hannah. She was only twenty-nine and expecting a baby within a couple months. The other was Latitia, Penn's daughter by his first wife, who had died five years earlier. Latitia was twenty-one years old, fresh and pretty. The tall young man who had come ashore with them was James Logan, Governor Penn's personal secretary.

Theo felt strange. He'd known all of them before his family came to the colony from England a year ago . . . but a year was a long time. And America was different from England, even though Pennsylvania was a British colony. And now, with Bernie's accident, he just didn't feel like talking with old family friends.

Nicole, on the other hand, had quickly overcome her shyness and was pestering the women with a lot of questions. "Are your clothes the latest styles from Europe?" she asked, eyes agog.

"Oh no," said Latitia with a smile. "Papa says a good Quaker shouldn't make a show of clothing."

Theo snorted softly. Maybe the governor and the two women weren't making a *show* of their clothing, but they seemed more finely dressed than most Quakers he knew. Certainly fancier than his own family. Though the Storys were not strict about wearing the plain, dark clothes of some Quakers, they avoided the frills and lace so many other colonists wore.

"But what about your shoes?" Nicole persisted. "I've never seen such high heels, and they have curved backs, as well."

Theo could have rolled over the gunwale with embarrassment right into the icy river. Calling attention to a grown woman's feet in public was just too rude. He looked at his mother, but Abigail Story seemed as interested in Latitia's answer as Nicole was. Theo smiled to himself. For once his mother wasn't grieving about Jessica. Maybe someday they would get over the loss of his baby sister.

As for Latitia, she pulled up her skirts far enough to show her shoe and turned her foot from side to side as she said, "Oh, these little things? They're just 'Louis' heels. Everybody in Europe is wearing them these days."

Theo couldn't help think that the heels would sink in the mud the first time it rained.

The longboat pulled alongside the *Canterbury*. As soon as everyone had scrambled on board, the captain ordered the anchor raised and the sails set to catch the stiff breeze that had arisen and would send them up the river to Philadelphia.

As the ship approached Philadelphia two hours later, everyone came back up on deck, even though the sharp, cold wind stung their faces. In spite of the chop the wind kicked up on the water, dozens of buckskin-clad Iroquois Indians came out in their canoes to greet the ship.

"I knew you were well-liked by the native people," said Thomas Story to the governor, waving a greeting at the canoes, "but I had no idea they considered you such a close friend . . . and after fifteen years! They've been bringing gifts for a fortnight—turkey, venison, pumpkins, corn, tobacco. Two chiefs are camped out on our yard. What did you do for them, William?"

The governor shrugged and turned both hands up. "I treated them fairly—just the way I would want to be treated."

Eager townspeople crowded the waterside, but as they got closer Thomas Story said to the governor, "Don't be surprised, sir, that there aren't more people here to greet you. Philadelphia is recovering from a severe epidemic of yellow fever." He looked over at his wife to make sure she wasn't listening and then continued in a low tone. "You probably haven't heard that we lost our little Jessica . . . just over a month ago now, it was."

"Oh, Thomas. I'm so very sorry," said William Penn, putting his hand on his aide's shoulder. Then he looked down at Theo. "I'm sure you miss your little sister deeply, too."

Theo nodded and looked across the water toward the town.

"Well," said the governor, "I can understand if the turnout is a little small." Then taking a deep breath, he added, "But it looks like a good many more homes have been built since I last saw this 'city of brotherly love.' How large is the town now?"

Theo's father seemed glad to move on to happier subjects. "Yes, larger indeed. There are over four hundred houses, and as you can see, many are brick and stone."

"I was surprised my cousin didn't come down to Chester," said the governor. "Is everything well with him?" Theo knew that the governor's cousin William Markam had been deputy governor in Penn's absence.

"I'm sure he and Mayor Shippen await us on the shore," said Thomas Story. Theo thought his father seemed to hesitate. "As far as I know, everything is in order. The people think well of Markham. But . . . to be honest, William, I'm not sure 'The Holy Experiment' you started is turning out quite like you expected."

Theo looked to the governor. All his life he had heard how William Penn had founded his colony on religious liberty and the faith that people would live responsibly if they were treated fairly. But the governor remained silent, gazing at the "city of brotherly love" as the ship dropped anchor and the passengers disembarked. Unlike the reception that morning in Chester, everything went smoothly in Philadelphia, and by evening the returning governor and his party were seated comfortably around the table in the Story home, a solid brick house built just the past year.

After the meal of roast chicken and winter squash, William Penn said, "Do you know the lad who was injured this morning?"

"Only slightly," said Theo's mother, Abigail. "He lives here in Philadelphia. I think Theo knows him somewhat, don't you, Theo?"

Theo looked down at his plate. "Yes, ma'am. His name's Bernie Bevan."

"Well," said the governor, "I'm concerned whether he needs financial assistance in recovering from his injuries. Is his father well employed?"

"His father's dead, sir."

"Hmm. Then I should make provision for his medical care. When was the last time you saw him, son?" asked the governor.

"This morning, sir."

"I understand that. This morning we all saw far too much of his poor—" He looked around the table at his wife and daughter and then continued. "I mean, I know you were there after the accident. But when did you see him before that?"

Theo swallowed. "Just before. Up . . . up by the cannons."

"Theo," said his mother sharply, "certainly you weren't involved in that foolish escapade."

"No . . . no. I didn't have anything to do with it."

"But you saw them preparing to fire that cannon?" His father took up the quiz.

Theo glanced around at all the adults staring at him. "I never thought something like that would happen," he protested. They weren't going to blame him, were they?

"Did you know Bernie was going to fire the cannon?" asked his father.

"Well, yes, sir. I guess so."

"You *guess* so? Why didn't you tell somebody if

you knew those boys were going to do something wrong?"

Theo started to say that he didn't know it was wrong, but then he remembered how Bernie had told him that the mayor had forbidden it. Still, it wasn't his business, was it? He remembered a phrase from somewhere in the Bible that seemed to fit. " 'Am I my brother's keeper?' "

A dark look crossed his father's face. Uh-oh, he was in big trouble now. He hadn't meant to be sassy. Then William Penn said softly, "Son, I think you better look up that Scripture before you quote it again."

Ever since William Penn had been in Pennsylvania the first time, work had slowly proceeded on Pennsbury Manor, a mansion suitable for the governor, large enough to receive his many guests and beautifully furnished. But it wouldn't be finished until spring, so the Penns settled temporarily into a fine slate-roofed house on Second Street between Chestnut and Walnut. Theo did not see the governor often, though his father worked with him nearly every day and often brought home stories of how the colony was adjusting to Penn's return.

Christmas came and went, as did New Year's Day 1700, bringing in a new century. At the end of January, Hannah Penn gave birth to a healthy baby boy they named John. Then one frosty afternoon in

February, William Penn stopped by the Story home and asked for Theo.

"How would you like to go visit your friend Bernie Bevan?"

Theo agreed instantly. He hadn't known Bernie had returned to Philadelphia. "Does that mean he's getting better?" he asked the governor as they walked across town to the Bevan house.

"To tell you plain and simple," answered the governor—he always spoke the plain and simple truth; that's why people trusted him—"the answer is no. He's not doing well at all. I've visited him every week down in Chester and thought he'd better be home with his mother for his last days."

Last days? Theo could hardly believe what the governor had said. Was Bernie going to die? If he had lasted this long, why wouldn't he live?

But when Theo saw Bernie, he knew the governor was right. Bernie looked only a shadow of his former self. Theo wanted to cheer up his friend, but he couldn't think of anything to say. It was Bernie who talked in a raspy, whispery voice about the good times they'd had the previous year: skating on the millpond, hunting in the woods, going to the Indian jamboree. While William Penn was talking to Bernie's mother, Bernie said slowly, "I guess you were the smart one, Theo, to get down off that hill and not mess with those cannons. How come you never told on us?"

Theo shrugged uneasily. He still hadn't looked up that verse like William Penn had told him to.

On the way home he said to the governor, "You remember that verse you told me to look up about being my brother's keeper? Do you know where it is in the Bible?"

"I think you'll find it in Genesis 4."

Theo liked the way the governor wasn't pushy. Some adults would have quoted the verse to you—or made you look it up and read it out loud—and then they'd give you a big lecture. But William Penn seemed willing to wait for him to find it on his own . . . or not. It was up to him.

That night he took the family Bible into his room and looked up the fourth chapter of Genesis by the light of his bed lamp. The verse he had quoted, verse nine, was Cain's answer to God as he tried to avoid accepting any responsibility for his missing brother, when actually he had killed him. Theo recoiled. No, that wasn't what he had wanted to be saying about Bernie. He hadn't killed Bernie . . . on the other hand, there was something he might have done to make a difference. He could have told someone what the boys were planning. He could have been his "brother's" keeper.

Theo grabbed the reins as William Penn's beautiful dappled gray horse skidded to a halt in front of the Story house. Penn loosened the ruffled white scarf at his neck. "I've just been out to Pennsbury Manor," he said sharply to Thomas Story. "Did you

know what's going on out there?"

"Well, I thought so. They've been working on your new house for fifteen years. When I saw it, it seemed almost ready for you to move in. Is that not so?"

"Of course it's so. The place is beautiful, but this gardener, this . . . this Hugh Sharp, has purchased three black slaves in my name to do the work! I have seen them working around the place several times, but I had no idea they were slaves. I cannot have that!"

"William, calm down. If Sharp doesn't know how to manage them, we can find someone else. Nothing's lost."

"No, no! It's not their work. The garden is beautiful—for this time of year, at least. But I cannot own slaves. It's wrong! But now what am I going to do? If I sell them, they will be someone else's slaves, and possibly be mistreated. What am I to do?"

"William, come in. Let's sit down and talk this out calmly. Theo, cool off his horse, then give it some oats."

When Theo returned to the house, his father was sitting in his armchair while the governor paced back and forth before the warm fireplace. "Then that's exactly what I will do," Penn was saying. "I will free the slaves and offer them the choice to stay on and work for me for a fair wage, or I will provide them with the tools and some land and money to start life on their own."

"Sounds good," said Thomas Story. "But I warn you. It is likely to create a fuss among the townspeople. They will think you are saying slavery is wrong, and no one likes being judged."

"No one likes being judged? But it's *wrong*, and they should be told so! There ought to be a law against this evil practice."

"Now, William," said Theo's father, "you know

31

that would never pass the Assembly. People want the freedom to live as they please. They would say such a law infringes on their rights."

"Rights! Everybody wants their *own* rights, but no one seems willing to accept the responsibility that goes with the liberty we enjoy here. What about the rights of those slaves? Don't they have any rights?"

"Well, you and I and a few other devout Quakers might agree that slavery is wrong," said Thomas Story, "but we can't *force* people to do right, can we? Isn't it an issue of morals and belief? Not a matter for law."

"But what's government for if not to organize and sometimes force people to do right?" complained Penn. "Some people would kill and steal if it were not for the law. And speaking of stealing, we still have a problem with pirates along our coast."

"Our people are not pirates."

"No, but some of them profit from trading with pirates. 'Live and let live,' they say. Everyone has come here for liberty, so the last thing anyone seems willing to do is make a law that infringes on someone else's 'liberty,' even if it is for the common good." Governor Penn clasped his head in his hands, producing a small cloud of white powder from his curls. "My 'Holy Experiment' seems to be unraveling, Thomas. I wanted to create a colony where *all* people could live in peace and brotherhood. The only thing that has not gone sour is my relationship with the Indians. At least they still love and trust me."

Theo had never seen William Penn so upset, pacing back and forth and preaching until he was red in the face. Suddenly, the governor noticed Theo standing in the doorway. He stopped with one hand on his hip, the other hand on his chin as he stared at Theo, but it was as though the governor was looking right through him, not really at him. Then Penn snapped his fingers at Theo. "Theo," he said, patting the pockets of his waistcoat as if looking for something, "go find your mother. I have something very important to show her and your father."

The governor had been so agitated that Theo went immediately to find his mother. When they returned to the sitting room, William Penn was opening an envelope and unfolding a letter.

"I'm sorry. In my concern about those . . . those slaves on my own property, I almost forgot this news from England. It arrived this morning." Penn handed the letter to Theo's mother. "It's the third paragraph that sadly concerns you, Abigail."

Chapter 3

Escaping Yellow Fever

W HAT IS IT, MOTHER?" Theo saw the worry spread across his mother's face.

"It's your grandfather," she said without looking up.

"What about Grandfather?" asked Nicole, who had just entered the room. She looked around at everyone present and said again, "What's the matter with Grandfather?" But when no answer came, her voice rose shrilly. "Why won't anyone tell me? What about Grandfather?"

 Abigail slowly folded the letter and replaced it in the envelope. "He's passed away," she whispered. "I must go back to England to help settle the estate."

"Not Grandfather!" wailed Nicole. "We can't lose Baby Jessica *and* Grandfather!"

Theo felt everything go tight inside. Baby Jessica ... Bernie ... his grandfather ... it was too much! Why was everything going wrong?

"O dear Lord," said Mr. Story, going to his wife's side. She leaned her head against him, and he held her quietly for a few moments. "But why must you go back, Abigail?"

William Penn answered. "It's the Whigs and the Tories—still bickering. That letter is from my lawyer. He had just heard of your father-in-law's death and thinks it would be best if Abigail returned. There is so much upheaval in the government right now that without a close family member present, she could lose the estate."

"But we can't go back right now. There's too much to do here."

"You are a tremendous help to me, Thomas, I won't deny it," said the governor. "But you need to do what is required for your family."

"No," said Mrs. Story. She spoke in a surprisingly resolute voice. "I will return with the children. You can stay here, Thomas, and help the governor. I may be in danger of losing my family's estate if I don't go back, but the governor is in danger of losing a whole colony if things don't get straightened out. We will leave as soon as possible."

"You can't do that," Thomas protested. "It took the governor two extra months to cross the North Atlantic because of winter weather—and some of the worst weather may yet be ahead. And why take the children?"

"Your husband has a point, my dear," Penn added. "Besides, I don't think you want to travel until this pirate trouble has been cleared up. Captain Kidd is scheduled for transport to England very soon to stand trial, but I would wait until he is safely on his way before heading out to sea. Who can tell what might happen? The politics in New York are unpredictable. Kidd might be released tomorrow."

"Then," said Mrs. Story, "I'll go as soon as the weather turns and this pirate you both seem to fear is out of the way. But I do want to take the children. They need me, and they may not have a chance to see their relatives again for many years."

Theo stood at the port railing of the *Loyal Tradesman*, looking across the water toward the faint line on the horizon that marked the northern tip of Long Island. It was the afternoon of their third day on board ship, and he was bored and restless. They hadn't seen another ship since before lunch. Would it be weeks before they saw land again?

His mind wandered to the events of the past month. On March 11, 1700, the frigate *Advice*, under command of Captain Robert Wynn, had sailed from New York for England with thirty-two pirate prisoners on board. Captain Kidd was securely among them. As the news spread, it seemed as though the people in the colonies heaved a collective sigh of relief. Now the seas around them would once again be safe for travel.

On April 3, after two weeks of calm weather and the promise of a mild spring, Bernie Bevan died from the injuries he sustained while firing the cannon. Theo and his family attended the sparse funeral. Two days later Abigail Story, Theodore, and Nicole departed from Philadelphia on the *Loyal Tradesman*. Theo could still see his father—standing on the dock, looking forlorn—and hear his final words: "God go with you!"

After sailing down the Delaware River and out of the bay, the ship had turned north along the Atlantic coast so they could catch the prevailing westerlies toward Europe.

"Look, did you see that?" Nichole appeared at Theo's elbow and pointed down at the waves not far from their ship.

"What? I didn't see anything."

"It was a huge dragonfly or a little bird. No, no. It looked more like a dragonfly. It was flying across the water until it hit a wave."

"Dragonfly! There're no dragonflies this far out."

"Yes, there was. I saw it. Look! There's another one."

This time Theo saw it, too, but it was no dragonfly. It was longer than his hand, and it had actually come up out of the water for sixty or seventy feet before it splashed into the top of a wave. In the next few minutes, they spotted several more of the strange creatures and were talking excitedly when the captain came walking by.

"Those are flying fish, children. Notice their front fins; they're nearly as long as their bodies." The captain stood with his head back and his shoulders square. "We seldom sees flying fish this far north, but down near the islands, you can see hundreds of them. If you leave a lantern out at night, you are liable to find several of them stranded on deck the next morning. They become a regular nuisance."

At that moment one of the sailors approached the captain and said something in a low voice. The two talked urgently and soon both walked away.

"Did you hear that?" hissed Nicole. "He said there's yellow fever on the ship."

"I didn't hear that."

"You weren't listening, then."

"Well, he wasn't talking to us, now, was he. I don't go around eavesdropping on other people's conversations, like somebody I know." Theo turned and walked away.

But Nicole ran after him and grabbed his jacket sleeve. "But it's yellow fever, Theo, right here on this ship! The captain said they had to separate the men from the rest of the crew or it would spread. I'm going to tell Mama."

Theo knew the news would upset his mother. Sure enough, Mrs. Story set off immediately to find the captain; Nicole and Theo trailed behind like two goslings. She found the captain by the helm and went right up the steps to the poop deck without asking permission.

"Captain, I understand there is yellow fever aboard. Is that so?"

"Mrs. Story, would you please keep your voice down," said the captain. "Nothing has been confirmed. A couple of my men aren't feeling well, and the ship's doctor is attending to them. If there is any serious illness, we will do everything possible to protect all of the passengers and, of course, my other crew members. Now, if you—"

"Everything possible is getting me and my children off this ship right now." Mrs. Story's voice rose sharply. "We lost one child to yellow fever already, and I will not endanger my other children. I want you to take us to New York immediately."

"I'm sorry, Mrs. Story. That's out of the question. I have a ship to run, and we are on our way to England. You will be put ashore with the rest of the passengers when we arrive there."

Mrs. Story pointed toward the western horizon. "Isn't that New York over there? That doesn't seem so far. You can take us there. We will pay for the time we have already been on your ship, but I will *not* stay a day longer."

Theo groaned inwardly. Didn't his mother know that passengers don't order the captain around? But the captain looked amused. "Be my guest, ma'am," he said, gesturing with an open hand toward the sea.

Theo's mother stamped her foot and turned her back to the captain, looking out over the sea on the starboard side of the ship. She held her hand up to her eyes and then suddenly turned back. "Captain, forgive me for being so . . . so insistent, but we lost our little Jessica to yellow fever less than six months ago. I beg you. There appears to be another ship approaching us from the northeast. Could you hail that ship and put us aboard? If there is yellow fever aboard this ship, I *must* get my children off . . . please."

The captain put his spyglass to his eye and studied the approaching ship for several moments. Finally he lowered the glass. "I will make you a deal, Mrs. Story. I will attempt to hail that ship and get you on board *providing* you promise not to say another word about yellow fever while you are here on the *Loyal Tradesman*. I cannot afford to have panic aboard my ship."

Mrs. Story's eyes filled. "Thank you, Captain! Agreed."

When the sleek black ship had come about and was approaching alongside the *Loyal Tradesman*, the captain turned to Mrs. Story. "I don't like the look of her, ma'am. Her name says she is the *Nighthawk*, but I'm not familiar with her. She flies a Dutch flag, but she's heavily armed for a nonmilitary ship."

"But she is headed toward New York, isn't she?" said Mrs. Story.

"Who knows?" The captain put his speaking trumpet to his lips and called, "Ahoy, *Nighthawk*. Who is your captain?"

The man who came to the rail of the other ship was not dressed as a ship's captain, but he responded quickly enough. "Ahoy to you, *Loyal Tradesman*. Permission to come aboard your ship, Captain? It's a shame to shout at each other like this."

"Now, isn't that nice of him," put in Mrs. Story. "He's offering to come over here. You won't even have to put your boat in the water, Captain. Bid him come."

The captain scowled at Theo's mother. "*I* am the captain of this ship, Mrs. Story, and *I'll* be issuing the orders, thank you," he said coldly. But he put the speaking trumpet to his lips and yelled across to the *Nighthawk*, "Permission granted!"

In a few minutes, three men from the *Nighthawk* had launched a small boat and soon were scrambling up the side of the *Loyal Tradesman*. Two of them were obviously common seamen, but Theo noticed that they began strolling around the deck, looking up at the rigging and down the hatches and at the cannons. Then, as the third man stepped forward to address the captain, Theo noticed a patch over his eye. "It's Dr. Patch!" he said with relief. "He's the doctor who helped Bernie when he got his arm blown off."

"You know this man?" said the captain, relaxing slightly.

"Aye," said the man with the patch. "I do recall, there in Chester. How is the lad?"

"He . . . died last week, sir."

"I'm mighty sorry to hear that, son. I did what I could." Dr. Patch turned to the captain. "Now, Captain, what can we do for you?"

The captain pulled a gold watch on a chain out of his pocket and scowled at it before replying. "We haven't much time. The first thing you can do is tell me who your captain is."

Dr. Patch glanced at one of his men, who was still snooping around, and then he lifted his three-cornered hat briefly. "I'm sorry, sir, but our captain is unavailable at the moment. Nevertheless, here I am at your service. Uh . . . certainly you didn't hail our ship just to ask about my captain, did you, Captain?"

"Of course not. We have some passengers—"

"He doesn't have the yellow fever, does he?" broke in Mrs. Story.

Theo held his breath. His mother had promised not to mention yellow fever again while on board the *Loyal Tradesman*. The captain was scowling at her, but no one else seemed alarmed.

"As a practiced physician," said Dr. Patch, "I can assure you that he is free from all disease save one."

Mrs. Story put her hand to her mouth. "And what's that?"

"Mortality, dear woman, mortality." He laughed. "Even the Good Book says we all must die once. Hopefully that will not be today since I'm not as ready as I'd like to be." He laughed at his own joke and turned to the captain. "So, my good man, what can we do for you?"

"I am not your 'good man.' I am the captain of this ship, and I don't think we need any—" began the captain.

"What you can do for us," broke in Mrs. Story, "is take me and my children aboard your ship and deliver us to New York."

"Well," said Dr. Patch, "we weren't going directly to New York—"

"Or Boston, then," said Mrs. Story. "Either place would be fine, and we are prepared to pay. I don't have much money with me, but I can assure you I have just inherited a very large estate in England. Money is no problem."

Dr. Patch grinned broadly. "How can I say no to such a determined and charming lady? We would be glad to take you and your children on board the *Nighthawk*." He swept off his hat in a bow. "We are at your service."

At just that moment, one of the *Nighthawk*'s sailors sauntered behind the captain and bumped him into Dr. Patch.

"Oh, please excuse me, I'm so sorry," said the sailor. He quickly brushed at the captain's uniform as though he had soiled it. "The roll of the deck must have caught me wrong."

Theo thought that was strange. The sea was calm, and the ship had not been rolling much at all. Then Theo noticed something else. The gold chain that had run from a button on the captain's uniform to his watch pocket was missing. Or had the captain put it in a different pocket?

The captain was obviously displeased. "Mrs. Story, I don't advise you traveling on the *Nighthawk*. I do not know the ship or its captain. . . ."

"But we know the doctor here, Captain," said Theo's mother. "There's nothing more to discuss. Please retrieve our luggage and . . ."

But Theo was not paying attention to what else

she said. He was watching Dr. Patch. Theo noticed a glint of gold between the doctor's fingers as he put his hand into his shirt. Was it a ring . . . or the captain's watch? But when the man's hand came back, there was no question. Dr. Patch wore no rings on that hand.

Theo was startled. He nearly cried out that Dr. Patch had taken the captain's watch . . . but he hesitated. His mother was so intent on getting off the *Loyal Tradesman*; would she be angry if he made a fuss over an old watch? He was shocked to see the doctor pickpocket the captain, but . . . did it matter all that much? Maybe Dr. Patch was a shady character, but he seemed to have a good heart. He had tried to help Bernie, hadn't he? And what did Theo know about the *Trademan*'s captain? The captain probably had his own faults. Maybe he drank too much or didn't pay his crew.

Theo shrugged and turned away. His mother wanted off the *Loyal Tradesman*—that was the important thing. Besides, the captain had left the chain hanging out, practically asking for it to be taken. He shouldn't be so careless.

Theo didn't have any more time to think about it before the *Loyal Tradesman*'s sailors had loaded their luggage into the longboat and were helping his mother and sister over the side. He scrambled after them and the boat pulled away.

Once on board the *Nighthawk*, the Story family was shown to the captain's quarters. "There are just a few things of our captain's that we'll be moving out of there," said Dr. Patch. "Then you will be welcome to all the comfort this poor vessel can provide, including a solid door so you do not have to worry about any of this rabble disturbing you." He waved the back of his hand at a crew that looked like they hadn't been near a bath for months.

"But where is your captain?" asked Mrs. Story as two muscular men dragged a heavy chest down the gangway from the captain's quarters and lowered it by means of ropes down into the ship's hold. "And the rest of your crew? You seem to have very few men."

Dr. Patch looked out across the sea as the *Nighthawk*'s sails caught the breeze and pulled away from the *Loyal Tradesman*. Finally he answered, "Our captain's not with us for this voyage. To tell you the truth, he's on another ship right now, but we hope to have him and a few of our other mates back with us before too long."

Chapter 4

Shiver Me Timbers

THERE," SAID DR. PATCH as he ushered the Storys down the short gangway off the quarterdeck and into the captain's cabin underneath the poop deck on the sleek *Nighthawk*. "You just make yourselves to home, and if there is anything you need, just call through this grating on the door."

The grating he spoke of looked like bars on a prison door to Theo, but then this was the captain's quarters, and he wouldn't want anyone breaking into his cabin and stealing his valuables—like whatever was in that heavy chest the sailors had moved below deck. Theo looked back. What was in that chest, anyway? Could the *Nighthawk* be transporting gold for some wealthy Dutchman? Or maybe it was the captain's personal treasure saved from years of trading in exotic foreign ports.

The beamed cabin, which ran the full width of the ship under the low poop deck, might have felt confining had it not been for the windows on both sides and to the rear. But through the glass, Theo could see that they, too, were barred. Whoever the captain was, he sure didn't want anyone to break into his quarters.

Mrs. Story, exhausted from the transfer ordeal, sat down on the berth even before the sailors finished bringing their trunks and luggage into the cabin. Theo headed straight for the padded bench under the rear windows and opened one of them. The tangy sea breeze chilled his face as he looked out at the distant *Loyal Tradesman*, no bigger now than the tip of his thumb on the horizon as it made its way toward England.

The cabin door thumped closed and the latch clicked when the sailors left. Finally they were alone.

"Where am I going to sleep?" asked Nicole from the high-backed captain's chair by the writing table.

"You can sleep here with me," said their mother as she lay back on the berth.

"But it's not even as big as a regular bed. How can two people sleep in it?"

"We'll manage. Come on over here and give it a try."

Soon mother and daughter were both asleep, cuddled up beside each other.

Theo closed the window and began exploring the captain's things. On one shelf he found a set of scales, a broken clock—at least it was not ticking—a mask that looked like it came from Africa, two candles, and a little tinderbox with flint and steel. Another shelf had several books, including a small New Testament and a copy of *Pilgrim's Progress* like the one his mother had been reading to the family at home. He got it down and found the place where they had been reading—the chapter in which Pilgrim and Hopeful had been captured by the Giant Despair. But before long he, too, fell asleep.

A tremendous explosion awoke Theo. Before he could remember where he was, the cabin was shaken by another blast and then another. Nicole began wailing in fright.

"Don't worry. Don't worry," said their mother, pulling Nicole close and looking around frantically. "It—it's probably only thunder. Yes, yes, we must've sailed into a storm."

Outside, men were yelling, and then they felt the ship crash into something, shaking the whole ship and throwing Theo off his bench onto the floor. The rear window swung open to reveal a deep blue sky of early evening, streaked with occasional pink clouds. "Th-that's no storm," he stammered as he got to his feet and staggered to the cabin door, but it wouldn't budge. Through the grating, however, he could see men running across the deck, some with cutlasses in their hands, others carrying muskets. But his view was restricted by the gangway so that he could see only a small part of the quarterdeck.

Another huge explosion shook the ship, and he saw the butt of a cannon recoil across his view.

"We're firing our cannons!" he yelled to his mother and sister. "We're at war!"

"War! But with whom?" asked Mrs. Story, moving swiftly to the door.

"I can't tell. I can't see the other ship."

Nicole was still whimpering. Theo started to say something, then held his tongue. He guessed if there ever was a time to cry, this was it!

He stepped aside so his mother could look through the grating and ran to the side of the ship where the fighting seemed to be happening. He struggled with the window until he got it open a few inches. Through this opening he could see the other ship silhouetted against a brilliant sunset. It was much larger than the *Nighthawk* and right alongside. Smoke was everywhere.

"What's happening?" begged Nicole. She had stopped her crying and come to his side, but there wasn't room for both of them to see out of the window.

There was a lull in the cannon blasts. "Several men from the *Nighthawk* have thrown grappling hooks into the rigging of the other ship and are boarding it," said Theo.

His mother joined them, having given up seeing anything through the door grating.

"Some of the men on the other ship are in uniform—they look like officers."

"What country are they from?" asked his mother.

"I can't tell. I can't see the flag, but they look like British sailors."

"British sailors? That can't be. Maybe they are French. Can you hear anyone speaking French?"

"No." Theo watched a minute more. "Our men are getting beaten back. There are just too many on the other ship."

"O Lord, have mercy. Don't let us be captured." Mrs. Story clasped her hands and held them to her mouth.

Again Nicole started to cry.

"The two ships are drifting apart, and some of our men are jumping into the sea and trying to swim back. Wait! . . . The other ship *is* flying a British flag. They're yelling 'Pirates' at us."

"Here, let me see." His mother pushed Theo aside. "Oh my," she said after a few moments, "I think we're on a pirate ship that has just attacked a British merchantman!"

She left the window and rushed over to their trunks. She opened one and began rummaging through their clothes. Theo resumed his position at the window and saw that some of the *Nighthawk*'s crewmen had been driven to the rail and were surrendering. By this time the two vessels had drifted forty feet apart, and the other ship began firing its cannons again at the *Nighthawk*.

"Here," said Theo's mother, shoving one of Nicole's

dresses into his hand. "Wave this out the window. If they see that women and children are here, maybe they will rescue us."

At that moment one of the cannonballs from the other ship must have hit the *Nighthawk* with a solid blow, because the whole ship shuddered. "Hurry," said Mrs. Story, "before they blow us out of the sea."

Outside, they could hear Dr. Patch yelling orders, and the *Nighthawk* began to pull away, leaving behind the men swimming toward it. The sound of cannon fire began to fade.

Abigail Story's face was white. "I guess that's that," she said, slumping into the captain's chair. "This is a fine fix. A pirate ship! What will we do now?"

After a few minutes of calm, broken only by the occasional order called by Dr. Patch, Abigail Story went to the door of their cabin and began pounding on it. "Open this door and let us out of here!" she yelled. Then after a few moments with no reply, "We will *not* be held prisoner. Dr. Patch, I insist that you open this door immediately. You had no right locking us in here!"

"Mighty sorry, ma'am" came the reply from Dr. Patch. It sounded like he was just above them, probably manning the helm. "We locked the door for your own protection during the attack. But now we have successfully repelled the enemy. You are again safe with us."

" 'Repelled the enemy' . . . 'safe with us'—what a liar," snarled Theo's mother in disgust. "If I'd known he was so dishonest, I never would have boarded this dreadful vessel."

A vision of Dr. Patch stealing the captain's watch came to Theo's mind like a ship out of a fog. *He* had known that Dr. Patch was dishonest, but he hadn't told anyone, not even his mother.

"Dr. Patch!" called Mrs. Story again. "I know you are pirates, and I demand that you release us from this . . . this cell immediately."

"I cannot do that, madam. We have suffered considerable damage during the exchange, and there is debris all over the deck. We have lost many a mate and are shorthanded. It will be some time before it is safe enough for you to come out."

"I can find my way around without tripping, thank you," said Mrs. Story. "Now, let me out!"

"It's not just the deck. There is broken rigging that could fall on you. You must trust us. We are working as fast as we can."

"I don't see anybody out there cleaning up the deck," she muttered to Theo and Nicole. "Wait, there's one man, but he's wounded and lying on his back." She raised her voice again. "Dr. Patch, at least let me come out and help you attend to your wounded."

After a few moments and a little shuffling above them, Dr. Patch unlocked the door. "Aye, ma'am. I could use a wee bit of ye help, but the children must remain inside. As I said, it be a matter of their safety. Now, watch ye step."

Theo and Nicole sat together in the darkening cabin listening to the creaking of the ship over the gentle roll of the sea. Finally Theo retrieved the candles and tinderbox and lit the candles.

It was dark when his mother returned. "What's happening?" Theo demanded.

"Are they pirates?" Nicole breathed, wide-eyed.

Mrs. Story sighed. "Yes, they are pirates, but Dr. Patch still won't admit it. They've lost all but five men, including Patch, and one of them is wounded— I don't think he'll make it. They've barely enough to sail this ship in the best of weather. There were three dead men on deck." She shook her head. "He sailed away and left his own men swimming in that cold water just to save himself. . . . He's a pirate, no doubt. The wounded man kept talking about Captain Kidd. I'm . . . I'm afraid this is the remnant of his old crew."

"What's going to happen to us, Mama?" wailed Nicole.

Mrs. Story sank down on the narrow berth and pulled both children close. "Only the Lord knows now, but I'm afraid they may have had plans for us from the beginning." She sucked in her breath. "I never should have mentioned my family's estate."

Chapter 5

Hidden Away in Bombay Hook

THE *NIGHTHAWK* SAILED SOUTH for two days. Theo and his mother and sister remained confined to the captain's cabin. Abigail Story guessed that Patch was taking them to some pirates' hideaway in the Caribbean islands. "Then they'll contact Thomas and demand a huge ransom for our freedom. But don't worry, children, your father will arrange to pay it, and he'll have Governor Penn's help, as well."

It was hunger that awoke Theo on the third morning before either his mother or sister. What little food they had been given was barely edible: hard tack, salt pork, and—after his mother complained—  a bowl of tasteless porridge. As quietly as possible, Theo got up and searched the cabin again.

This time, in the back of a small cabinet, he found a tin of sweet biscuits. He took the tin back to his bench and began munching. He opened the rear window and recoiled from the glare of the newly risen sun. It was too bright, shining straight in the window and reflecting off the water. But . . . that meant they had changed course.

Theo frowned. They were no longer sailing south, they were going due west . . . toward land, and certainly toward the colonies, because they couldn't possibly be anywhere near the West Indies yet.

He closed the rear window against the glare and went to the starboard window on the right side of the ship. If he could just get it open far enough, he might be able to see ahead a little, possibly even see land. But when he opened it, there was no need to look ahead. Through the small opening he saw a flat sea and not more than three miles distant, a flat, sandy point backed by a low tree line.

"Mama, Mama, wake up!" he whispered urgently, crossing to the port side and opening that window. On the left side, they were not nearly so close, but in the far distance, he could see another line of low, white sand dunes. "Mama, wake up! Look out that window."

Theo went back and joined her. After a few minutes she said, "I think we're going around a point. See, the water opens up again."

"But look how smooth and light-colored the water is, Mama. It's not the open sea. I think we're entering a bay."

They crossed to the port side. "See, Mama? There's another point to the south."

"Yes," she said quietly. "We *are* entering a bay, and I think it is Delaware Bay. That must be Cape Henlopen, and to the north, that was Cape May. Oh, Theo! We're going home!"

The bay was large and they soon lost sight of the northern shore. Three hours later, however, they heard Dr. Patch giving orders to lower the sails until the *Nighthawk* was barely creeping through the water. The ship was now within a couple hundred yards of the shore to the port, and the bay seemed to be narrowing. "I can see the far shore up ahead," Theo reported from his post by the starboard window.

"Why are we stopping?" asked Nicole. "Let me see!"

Mrs. Story had no sooner said, "I don't know," when the ship began to come about and head directly toward the white sand dunes and low trees.

"You don't think Dr. Patch is going to beach it, do you, Mama?" asked Theo.

"I have no idea what that crazy man intends."

But the answer to Theo's question became apparent a few minutes later as the *Nighthawk* slipped between the sand dunes and made its way slowly up a river that dumped into Delaware Bay. High sand dunes rose from the banks on both sides, with scattered tufts of grass and clumps of stunted willow bushes dotting them here and there. Behind the dunes they began to see the tops of cottonwood trees.

"Look lively, me hardies," they heard Dr. Patch shouting. "We need more hands. Get that boy up here on deck!"

A moment later the door to their cabin was unlocked, and a tall, muscular black man with a shaved head and a gold earring as large as a woman's bracelet—it probably had been a bracelet at some point—motioned to Theo. "Step to it, lad. The doc needs you to swing the lead." His English was clear, and he had a small gold cross hanging from a gold chain around his neck. Theo guessed he might be an escaped slave.

But Theo held back. "Swing the lead? I don't know anything about swinging lead."

"You'll learn soon enough. Now, get out here."

Even though the morning was still chilly, the man wore no shirt. His pants were torn off at the knees, and around his neck hung a beautifully embroidered strap with a pistol tied to each end. Reluctantly, Theo followed him to the bow of the ship. Debris from the battle still littered the deck, though most of it had been pushed overboard. At the front of the ship, Theo looked up. There, flying from the headstay, was a black flag with a skull and crossbones, the "Jolly Roger" of a bold pirate ship. There was no doubt now.

The bald-headed pirate handed Theo a piece of lead the size of his fist to which was attached a coil of line with knots tied every so often.

"Listen sharp, boy. Give yourself about two feet of line, swing the lead around like a slingshot, and toss it ahead of the ship thirty feet or so. When it hits the bottom, you hang on to the line and keep it taut until the ship is right over it. Then pull it up quick-like, counting the knots as they come out of the water. Each knot equals one fathom. When the lead is in hand again, you sound off the number loud enough for Doc to hear you, and then repeat the whole thing. You got it?"

"But why—?"

"So we won't hit a sandbar," the man growled

impatiently. "If we go aground, we may never get her free."

The black man left Theo and went back to help his mates with the lines controlling the two sails that were still aloft, giving the ship its forward momentum. Up in the rigging was a man with a bald head and a bushy red beard. Theo could see tattoos on his arms that looked like fish scales. Another man stood on the deck holding one of the sheets, the ropes that adjusted the sails. He wore a blue-and-white checkered scarf on his head and a large, drooping black moustache.

"Quit gawking, lad," yelled Dr. Patch. "You swing that lead like Cobo told you. I want to hear you. You're going to have to earn your grub."

Theo swung the lead as he had been shown and counted the knots when he pulled it up. "Four," he called and turned to see if Dr. Patch had heard him.

"Don't be lookin' at me, boy. You stick to business. Throw it back out there."

Theo threw it out and pulled it up. Again it was four. And again. Then it was three.

"You sure?" yelled Patch. "Do it again, quick."

Theo obeyed and yelled back, "Three."

Immediately, the black man whom Patch had called Cobo ran forward and made ready to drop the anchor. "You stay clear," he said to Theo. "If that line whips around your leg, it could take it clean off. Just you keep swingin' that lead."

"Where are we?" Theo asked casually.

Cobo threw Theo a sharp look. "Never you mind

where we are. That's our business."

Theo wasn't about to give up that easily. "But that was Delaware Bay back there," he said, more confidently than he felt.

The ruse worked. "So what if it was. We can't take any chances on getting spotted out there. Pretty soon the *Nighthawk* will be tucked so snug in her nest that nothin' but sea gulls'll be able to find her." He laughed. "Now, look sharp there, boy. Toss it over that way once."

"Three!" yelled Theo a moment later.

"That was less than three!" Cobo yelled back to Patch. Then to Theo he growled, "Boy, you gotta count only what comes out of the water."

Dr. Patch yelled orders to the other two pirates, and suddenly the sails went loose and began flapping in the wind. The *Nighthawk* glided to a stop, then slowly began drifting back with the current while Patch spun the wheel furiously to keep it straight. He shouted again, and the sails filled with wind once more until the ship began to creep forward again, though this time Patch guided it slightly toward the other bank.

These delicate maneuvers continued for an hour while Patch skillfully piloted the *Nighthawk* a mile or more up a river that was no more than two hundred feet wide.

"What happened to the fifth pirate?" Theo asked.

Cobo scowled at him. "What do you mean, pirate? Who said we were pirates?"

"I'm talking about the wounded man . . . the one

my mother helped," Theo added quickly.

"Joey." Cobo nodded. He looked out at the slowly passing sand dunes for several seconds. "Joey was a good mate, but he just didn't make it." Cobo took a deep breath that expanded his muscular chest like a smithy's billows. "S'pose we'll all be joinin' him in Davy Jones's locker before long."

Theo shrugged. So much for trying to make casual conversation. He threw the lead once more and called out the number.

Finally they came to a bend, and once they were around it, the doctor called out to his sparse crew, "See that big cottonwood tree on the north bank? When we come abreast, tie her off. I think this should be far enough."

"Aye, aye," said the pirate near Theo.

Slowly Dr. Patch eased the ship over to the side, just past the cottonwood tree, and then gave orders to lower the sails and drop anchor.

"Cobo," called Patch once the black pirate had secured the anchor, "get aloft and see if we're well hidden."

"Why can't Red do it? He's already up there."

" 'Cause Red's busy furlin' that sail."

"Who made him captain?" mumbled Cobo, but Theo was amazed at how fast the big man climbed up the rigging. Finally the pirate found a foothold near the top of the main mast and studied the landscape in all directions. Then he called down, "I can see one small patch of water over yonder, but no one's going to see us here."

"Good," said Patch. "Get her tied off, mates."

Theo stayed out of the way, and when no one seemed to notice that they had not locked him back in the cabin, he sat down behind the longboat out of their sight. His thoughts scrambled. Maybe this was his chance to escape. Maybe when night came he would be able to release his mother and sister.

The pirates lowered a dinghy into the river and then used it to haul a rope from the stern of the ship to the huge cottonwood tree. Then they took a second rope with a small anchor on it from the stern out into the river to prevent the ship from drifting too close to the bank.

While they were doing this, Theo climbed over the gunwale of the longboat and tumbled into the bottom. No one would see him there unless they deliberately looked in.

Having secured the ship, the four pirates gathered back on the deck of the *Nighthawk*. Theo peeked over the edge of the longboat. The men were sharing a loaf of hard bread and some cheese while they passed around a bottle.

Theo's stomach ached for their bread and cheese. If they had bread and cheese on board, why hadn't they given any to his mother and sister and him during the past couple days? But in spite of his hunger, he remained silent.

"I want to explore what's upriver," said Patch. "We don't want to be surprised by any settlers."

"You don't have to worry 'bout the folks along Dona's River," said Cobo. "They understand what side their bread is buttered on. Ain't that right, Jerry?" Cobo cut a slice of cheese with a long, thin knife and handed it to the pirate with the drooping black moustache.

Jerry nodded as he took the cheese.

"What do you mean?" asked Patch.

Jerry "humphed" in derision. "Captain Kidd traded with all the colonists round here. You know that, Doc. All you have to do is show them a few coins and they'll keep their mouths shut."

"All the same," said Patch, "I want to know who's near us. Besides, we've got to find a way to get word to Mr. Story up in Philadelphia that we've got his wife and kids."

Peering over the edge of the longboat, Theo sucked in his breath.

"You really think he'll trade Captain Kidd for them?" said Red.

"He'll trade money for them," suggested Jerry.

"Yeah, but we want the *captain*," said Cobo, suddenly stabbing his dagger into the deck, "our real captain."

Patch eyed him for a moment, nodded, and then said, "Whether or not we can work out a deal for Kidd all depends on how much influence Governor Penn has back in England," said Patch. "But it's worth a try."

Theo slid back down into the bottom of the longboat. So *that* was the pirates' plan. They weren't after money so much as the release of Captain Kidd. Theo buried his head in the crook of his arm. With

Captain Kidd in England, it would take months to arrange such a deal . . . if it could be arranged at all. And with all the furor over piracy lately, that wasn't likely.

But what name did Cobo give this river? . . . Dona's River. He had to remember that. And he had to get his mother and sister out of the cabin and make their escape tonight. It might be their only chance!

Chapter 6

Captives 'Neath the Jolly Roger

G ET THAT LONGBOAT IN THE WATER," said Dr. Patch. "Dover Tavern's gotta be around here somewhere."

Theo raised his head and peeked over the edge of the longboat. He had to find another hiding place! If he could get to one of the cannons, he might duck down behind it, or maybe he could sneak up on the poop deck. Cobo might be tall enough to see him up there, but not the other pirates if he kept low. And there was some kind of a locker up there; maybe he could hide behind it. But how could he get there?

"We been workin' like dogs sailing this ship with only four hands on board," complained Red. "How 'bout a break? There's plenty of time to explore tomorrow."

"Yeah," said Cobo. "Let's take a vote on it." He looked at Dr. Patch to see if he would make any objection.

"If that's the way you lads want it," said Patch. "Who's for explorin' now?"

Theo could just see the men where they sat on the deck in the afternoon sun. Jerry started to join Dr. Patch in putting his fist toward the center of their little circle, but when he saw the frowns on Cobo and Red's faces, he withdrew it.

"So who's opposed?" said Cobo as he put his fist in, the gold cross swinging out from his broad chest as he leaned over.

Red's fist went down decisively, followed a moment later by Jerry's.

Red leaned back against the mainmast and crossed his tattooed arms. "Looks like we do it tomorrow. Who's in for a game of cards? Fetch us another bottle, eh, Jerry? We need some refreshment."

Theo sighed quietly. For the time being, he was safe.

The sun set, and the pirates brought out a lantern and continued playing cards and drinking. It apparently didn't occur to them that their captives might be hungry, but for once, Theo didn't mind. The less notice the pirates took of them, the greater the chance they wouldn't miss him being out of the cabin.

When the last twilight had faded from the star-spangled sky, Dr. Patch said, "I'm turning in, lads," and pulled himself to his feet with a grunt.

"Me too," said Cobo and followed him to the crew hatch.

Jerry got up and staggered toward the front of the ship, where he curled up on a folded sail.

Theo watched Red for a few minutes, until he realized that the pirate had fallen asleep where he sat, leaning against the mainmast. Theo scanned the deck. Why hadn't one of them blown out the lantern? Its light was soft, but it was enough to make it hard for him to move about the deck freely. The pirates would be able to see him if they woke up. But he couldn't worry about that now. Who knew how much time he would have before one of them woke up?

The boy climbed out of the longboat and made his way quietly to the gangway leading to the door of the cabin where his mother and sister were confined. Its dark shadows, at least, gave him some cover.

"Mama," he whispered, rapping lightly on the door.

She was at the grating in a moment. "Theo! Where have you been?"

"I've been waiting for them to go to sleep. They forgot to lock me up, but now we've got to get away."

"Get away? But where are we?"

"Heard 'em say Dona's River," Theo grunted, pulling on the door handle, but it didn't budge.

"Patch has the keys," whispered his mother.

"No, I think Cobo has them. He's the one who let me out this afternoon, and I never saw him return them to the cap—I mean, Dr. Patch. Besides, there's something going on between them. They don't like each other very much." He pulled with all his might on the door, but it did no good. "There's got to be another way to get this open."

Theo turned back down the gangway and looked for something on the deck to pry the door open. Some kind of a bar, or maybe a . . . and then he saw it— Cobo's dagger sticking in the deck between the lantern and the sleeping Red.

"O Lord," Theo said under his breath, "don't let him wake up."

Slowly Theo crept toward the center of the deck, hiding first behind the water barrel and then the capstan, but after that it was open deck between him and the mainmast, where Red slept. He decided to work his way around Red so that he approached him from behind, with the mast between himself and the pirate.

It was a good plan, but he no sooner got himself into this new position than Red stirred. Theo froze, but in trying to hold himself perfectly still, he realized that he was shivering. He hadn't noticed how chilly and damp the night air had become. It took all his concentration to remain still.

When Red had settled back into a relaxed position for several minutes, Theo crept forward but didn't see a broken pole that had been left on the

deck after the earlier battle. His foot caught it, and
the thing went spinning toward Red while Theo

stumbled to catch his balance. In the quiet night, broken by nothing louder than a distant bullfrog or the occasional creaking of the ship as it gently moved in the river's current, the clattering and thumping of the spinning pole on the deck of the *Nighthawk* sounded like a rock wall tumbling down.

Red sat up and rubbed his beard as Theo ducked behind the mainmast, not three feet away from the pirate. Then Red stood up and walked rather unsteadily to the bulwarks on the far side of the ship. He stood there at the side of the ship, weaving back and forth for a moment, and then Theo could hear the quiet sounds of water streaming into the river. Soon Red turned around and rubbed his head as though it ached as he made his way back to the mast and sat down. After a moment he reached out and pulled Cobo's dagger from the deck. He used it to extend his reach so that he could pick up the lantern with the tip of its blade. He brought it to himself and then blew out the light.

The deck was dashed into total darkness. Theo's taut muscles relaxed. At least he wasn't so visible any longer. But now he realized that he didn't know for certain where the dagger was. Was Red still holding it? Had he stabbed it back into the deck or just dropped it? Theo peeked around the mainmast, but he couldn't make out any shapes.

He had to keep calm. In a few minutes his eyes would adjust to the dark. He slowly lowered himself to his hands and knees. He wasn't going to risk tripping over anything else on the deck. From the lower perspective he could make out various silhouettes against the purple sky. And then, if he wasn't looking right at things, he began to recognize shapes against the light-colored wood of the deck.

Was Red asleep again? Why didn't the guy snore like other men? Theo was just about to start crawling toward the rear of the ship when he looked back one more time and the dull glint of the knife blade lying on the deck caught his eye. Did he dare move toward it? Or should he just get out of there?

Slowly he reached out and crabbed his way closer until his hand clutched cold steel. He retrieved it and slid the sharp blade down inside his belt at the back of his trousers. He crawled away without Red so much as stirring.

At the door of the cabin he worked furiously with the dagger, first of all trying to pick the lock, and then, when that failed, he tried to pry open the door. Suddenly the blade snapped in half.

"What happened?" his mother whispered, hearing the pop and his grunt.

A sob gripped Theo's throat so that he couldn't answer. Had he wasted their only chance? If he couldn't pick the lock or force the door open, what other way was there to free his mother and sister?

Finally he took a deep breath. "I broke the blade. I don't know what we're going to do."

"Don't worry, Theo. We're all still safe." Her fingers touched his hand gently through the window grate. "Our God will look after us."

✧ ✧ ✧ ✧

"Theo? Boy? Where are you?" It was Cobo's stern voice.

Theo looked at the broken dagger that he had dropped in the bottom of the longboat. Would the pirate see it? He sat up.

"Oh, there you are," Cobo said. "Climb on out of there. The day's a-wastin'. You want your mama and sister to get something to eat, don't you? I'm sure not going to serve them."

Theo quickly climbed out of the longboat so Cobo wouldn't come and investigate where he had slept. Cobo hadn't seemed at all surprised that he wasn't locked up in the cabin. It was as though he didn't care.

"There," Cobo said, "take that pan of cornmeal. It's got bacon bits in it. You can have that loaf of bread and jug of water. Oh, and there're some limes for you. You each better eat one of those so you won't get scurvy. No tellin' how much longer you'll be on ship's rations."

Theo followed Cobo back to the cabin, where the pirate unlocked the door and ushered him inside. "When you get done, give me a call so you can empty your slop bucket. Gotta put things shipshape around here."

Mrs. Story had been sitting by the window reading the ship's small New Testament. She got up and approached Cobo. "Do you read, sir?"

"Yes, ma'am." He grinned widely. "I learned back

74

in Carolina."

"Well, then, you might read this." She thrust the New Testament at him. "It might do you some good."

Cobo took the book and looked at it a moment, then held out his gold cross. "My mama was a Christian."

"You can't inherit a place in God's family. You have to choose it for yourself."

Cobo shrugged but left with the book.

When Theo had finished breakfast and was let out of the cabin to take care of the cleanup duties, he saw that the longboat had been lowered into the water, and the small sail had been unfurled and made ready for travel. He tried to get into a position so that he could look into the boat and see if the broken dagger was visible, but he couldn't see it.

"You've seen a longboat before," growled Dr. Patch. "Go on. Get back in your cabin. We're going to be taking a little journey, and we need to get underway."

"We'll let you and your sister out this afternoon when we return," said Cobo. He seemed sorry that they had to be locked up again.

"Maybe your mother, too," said Jerry. "Leastwise long enough to get some exercise. We want to be hospitable to our guests." He grinned, and Theo saw for the first time that he had two gold teeth right in the front.

The pirates returned in the late afternoon and immediately unlocked the door to the captives' cabin. Theo and Nicole came out eagerly, but Mrs. Story hung back, uncertain what the pirates had in mind.

"I'm going to Dover tonight," Red announced. He and Jerry had set to work cleaning the remaining debris off the deck while Dr. Patch carried supplies from the longboat to the ship's crew hatch. But Cobo sat down on a coil of rope on the deck and pulled out the New Testament and proceeded to read it.

"I'm going, too!" Jerry hissed once Dr. Patch was below deck. "You think Doc will allow that, Cobo?"

Cobo looked up from his reading. "Allow? It's not for him to allow or object. But tonight Red and I are going, so you better stay here with Doc."

"Who decided that?" Jerry fumed.

By this time Mrs. Story had come out onto the deck and was leaning against the ship's bulwarks with her face turned toward the west. She brushed her hair back from her face with her hands as though she was drinking in all of the afternoon's remaining sunshine.

"Mama," said Nicole, bouncing on tiptoe beside her mother, "they brought potatoes and onions and carrots and all kinds of things."

"You must be mistaken, dear. Where would they get things like that in this wilderness?"

But Cobo had overheard her. "You'd be surprised, Mrs. Story. We can always find some God-fearin' colonists happy to sell us fresh foodstuff . . . for the right price, that is." He laughed. "Good food, good drink . . . why, this very evening me and Red are fixin' to head over to a tavern sittin' right here in the middle o' nowhere for a little refreshment."

"Why don't you come along with us, Mrs. Story?" said Red slyly. "Can't take your kids, though, 'cause if me and Cobo drink too much, we wouldn't want you runnin' off."

Mrs. Story looked startled. Theo knew she was thinking this might offer an opportunity to escape or at least get help.

"Shut up, Red." Cobo shook his head and looked guiltily down at the Bible in his hand. "Don't pay any attention to Red, Mrs. Story. He's just joshin' you. I'm afraid you'll have to stay on board the *Nighthawk*."

The dispute over who could go to Dover Tavern that night and who would stay watch on the *Nighthawk* was settled by drawing lots. Red lost, and he was none too happy. Once the other three got into the dinghy and rowed across the river to the south bank where they found a trail leading over the dunes, Red shut the captives in their cabin without any supper and locked their door. They could hear him cursing and stomping around on deck, and sometimes through the grating in their door, they saw him with a bottle, drinking hard.

The next evening the same dispute arose, but Mrs. Story was quick to speak up. "Before you get to quarreling over who goes away to get drunk and who must stay here to get drunk, do you think you could give us our food?"

"Didn't they get anything to eat last night?" Dr. Patch challenged Red.

Red shrugged a sorry-but-I-couldn't-help-it look.

"I've a mind to make you stay here again tonight," Patch snapped. "They have to be in good health for us to get our demands."

Red tipped back his bald head so that his red beard stuck out and he was looking down his nose at Dr. Patch. "You just try to keep me here, and you'll lose your gizzard." His hand had smoothly moved to the handle of the dagger that he wore in his red sash.

"Here, now," interrupted Cobo, coming between the two men with his hands outstretched. "We don't need any of that. Of course Red's going tonight. We're all going."

"No, we can't—" began Patch.

"We're all going tonight, and they are getting their supper. Jerry, stir them up some salmagundi so we can get out of here."

"But what about . . . ?" Patch was pointing toward the Story family.

"They'll be as snug as sixteen men on a dead man's chest. Look. All you gotta do is keep Mama locked up—the kids ain't going anywhere. Nobody could go anywhere anyway with all those swamps and sand dunes in that wilderness out there."

"Gotta keep 'em all locked up," Dr. Patch muttered, but Cobo had taken charge to keep Red from using his dagger, so the doctor soon fell silent. And when the pirates later left in their overloaded dinghy, Theo was sitting on the poop deck at the very

78

stern of the ship, fishing with a string and a home-made hook.

Had Cobo left him free by accident or to prove that he was in charge now and could do as he pleased? Theo figured it was the latter, because not long before sending his mother and sister to their cabin, Cobo had called him down for his bowl of salma-gundi, the tasty seafaring stew of chopped meat, eggs, anchovies, onions, and carrots. Theo had taken it right back to his fishing spot, so Cobo must have been aware that Theo wasn't in the cabin.

When the pirates had disappeared over the first dune, Theo rushed down to his mother and sister. "They're gone," he called through the grating. He pulled at the door to see if it might have been left unlocked. No such luck. "I'm going to see if I can find something to open this door."

"Hurry, Theo. And be careful—they might come back."

Chapter 7

A Thump in the Night

THEO HEARD HIS MOTHER'S WARNING that the pirates might return soon, but he went straight to the hatch leading to the hold. He had to find a way to free his family.

In the gloom belowdecks he discovered berths for the crew, a small galley, another officer's cabin, and an open storage area with kegs of hardtack, salt pork, water, and rum . . . and the recently acquired foodstuff. He then found the magazine room with kegs of gunpowder, cannonballs, grenades, and other weapons. Briefly he considered trying to fight the pirates when they returned. Maybe with a grenade or one shot from a swivel gun he could sink their little dinghy before they boarded and then hold them off with a blunder-buss or a brace of pistols. But he knew that was foolish thinking. They needed to escape.

What he didn't find, however, were the keys for the captain's quarters or even a carpenter's chest that might hold tools he could use to break into the cabin.

Theo knew he had to hurry. If the pirates caught him belowdecks, they'd lock him up for sure. But he had only explored the aft portion of the ship. There was a solid bulkhead that separated the forward half of the ship from where he stood. He looked up at the hatch. To go forward was to be farther from his escape route in case he heard someone coming aboard. Did he dare risk it?

He went forward and pushed open the thick door in the bulkhead. All was dark ahead, too dark to find anything. He stepped back and found a lantern hanging from a beam. But to light it, he had to waste more time searching for a match, which he finally found in the galley.

So much time was passing. He looked up through the hatch and realized that the sky was getting dark. But he couldn't stop now. He went through the bulk-head door into the main hold. A rat scurried for safety behind some large bales of fine-looking cloth and other trade goods. There were several large sea chests, as well as many huge barrels held securely in place by ropes.

And then Theo spied *the* chest, the one the pi-rates had removed from the captain's quarters. It was not nearly so large as the other chests, but it was obviously much stronger, built to carry a heavy cargo. Copper bands strapped the chest and reinforced the corners. As he approached it, he realized that it was not quite as large as he remembered, but when he kicked it a little with his toe, it was like kicking an anvil.

Theo held the lantern down to examine it more closely, and then he realized that the lock hung loose. Someone had failed to reclose it.

He looked around the dark hold as though he feared someone might be standing there watching him. Then he knelt down, removed the lock, and raised the hasp. But the lid was so stuck that he had to put down the lantern and use two hands to open it. From within there was a glint that caused him to catch his breath. Almost reverently he picked up the lantern.

And then on the ship's hull there was a distinct thump.

Theo froze.

The thump came again, softer this time but followed by a scraping sound as something slid along the side of the ship. The pirates must have returned! How long had he been down there in the hold? It didn't seem that long, but Theo didn't stop to try to figure it out. He closed the lid, replaced the lock, and then blew out the lantern almost in one motion. Should he hide there in the hold or try to make it up onto deck?

He looked up and could make out a very faint

square line of light around the cargo hatch. Maybe if he hid in the cargo hold and someone came down the crew hatch looking for him, he could climb up through the cargo hatch. No. He couldn't risk it. It was almost certainly fastened.

Quietly he moved toward the bulkhead door, taking care not to trip over anything. It creaked as he opened it, but he had to get through. He climbed the steep steps up to the hatch until he could just peek over the edge. A sea fog had rolled in under a moonlit sky and cast the deck in floating shadows of soft silver and black, but Theo could make out no human figure.

Still, there *had* been two distinct thumps against the outside of the hull. Could they have come from an old log drifting down the river? No, no, as he thought about how the ship sat in the river, the scraping sound had gone upstream. It had not been made by something floating downstream.

Why would the pirates be so quiet coming aboard? Maybe they were too drunk to climb out of their dinghy. Theo climbed out of the hatch and quietly moved across the hazy quarterdeck and down the gangway. "Mama!" he whispered at the cabin door, but she did not answer.

Something clattered to the deck near the bow of the ship and then rolled aft, bumping into things along the way. It did not take Theo long to decide it was a musket ball, probably left over from the attack on the merchantman. But why would it dislodge in the quiet of the night with almost no noticeable

movement to the ship from the river's current? There had to be someone else aboard the ship. There was no other explanation.

Slowly Theo crept along the gangway, peering into the fog for a figure or a shadow of someone moving on the deck. Just as he reached the corner, a human shape swung around it and crashed into him. He yelled in fright, and another voice yelled just as loudly.

Both Theo and the other person were gasping for air. As Theo tried to make out who had bumped into him, he could see sweat glistening on the other person's body. It was a man . . . no, a boy . . . naked from the waist up, about his own size and build. But he had something dark standing up on his head that looked like a strange hat.

It was an Indian—a boy about his own age, and he did not wear a hat. His hair was cut in Mohawk style, shaved on the sides, leaving a tall, bushy strip down the middle.

Theo eased his way out of the gangway onto the quarterdeck. The Indian backed up slowly, keeping a safe distance. Finally Theo pointed at him and said, "Who . . . are . . . you?" not knowing whether the boy understood English.

But the other boy responded in English with only a slight accent. "I am Tammany. Are you one of the pirates?"

"No," said Theo quickly. "We . . . I mean, I am being held captive on this ship." He was not yet ready to reveal that his mother and sister were also on the ship, but his precaution was useless because at that moment his mother began calling through the door.

"Theo! What is it? Are you all right?"

"I'm fine, Mama. We have an Indian guest."

"An Indian! Oh, Theo, I knew I shouldn't have left you out there all alone tonight."

"Don't worry, Mother. He's about my age." Theo turned to the boy. "My name is Theo. How . . . how did you get on the ship?"

The Indian boy led him to the side of the ship. Theo could make out the dim outline of a dugout canoe tied to the rope ladder hanging over the side.

So the canoe had caused the thumping and scraping alongside the ship.

"I need help getting off the ship," Theo said suddenly. "Would you help me escape from these pirates?"

"I could guide you to Dover Tavern."

Theo snorted. "I don't think that would work. That's where the pirates are, and it sounds like some of the people around here are so friendly with them that they'd probably return me to the pirates rather than help me escape."

"My people would help you," said Tammany. "You need to go to Philadelphia and see the English governor, William Penn. My father knew Governor Penn before I was born. I've been to Philadelphia many times."

"How far is that?" asked Mrs. Story through the grating.

"Four days, maybe more, maybe less."

"Oh, Theo. I don't think it would work for you to go by yourself," said Theo's mother. "As soon as the pirates return, they will figure out that you've gone for help. Then they might move the *Nighthawk* before anyone could come back and rescue Nicole and me! This time they might sail all the way to the Caribbean, and then no one could find us."

Theo's heart sank. His mother was right. "We've got to find a way to get everyone out of that cabin when the pirates are gone," he said. "It's our only hope."

His mother's voice sounded tired. "I . . . I think that's what they're counting on. If they keep even one of us in here, they know the others aren't going to run off. And they're right. We can't take a chance on getting separated."

"There's got to be carpenter tools on this ship," said Theo. "Tammany, come with me. We've got to find them. It's the only way to break them out."

Tammany stood guard as Theo went belowdecks again and made another search, this time with the lighted lantern. But there were no saws, pry bars, hammers, or anything to be found that might cut through the door. Again, Theo looked in the magazine room. Could he use one of the grenades to blow the door open? It was a thick door and a strong lock, carefully designed to resist such efforts. Besides, there was too great a chance that the explosion might injure his mother and sister.

He came to the steps below the hatch. "I can't find anything," he said in despair. "Maybe we can trick 'em into leaving us all free some—"

"Shh!" interrupted Tammany. "The pirates are returning. I hear them coming through the dunes. I must go now."

"Wait," whispered Theo as he blew out the lantern and hurried up the steep steps. But by the time he reached the deck, the young Indian was over the side and in his canoe. "Come back tomorrow night," Theo whispered, but he had no way of knowing whether Tammany heard him before he drifted downriver as silent as a leaf on the water.

Theo strained his eyes to see the far shore. Then he heard the pirates laughing and singing some drinking song as they stumbled through the sand and clambered into their dinghy. He, however, didn't wait to welcome them aboard but made his way to the pile of folded sails and lay down as though he were asleep.

Three days passed in much the same fashion. In the late afternoon, the pirates would head off to Dover Tavern, but in the middle of the night, they would return drunk and rowdy to sleep until late the next morning. On two of the nights, all three Storys were locked in the cabin. On the third night, Cobo left Theo free again. But what good was it when his mother and sister were still locked up? Tammany came by each night to see them. His company was encouraging, and he brought them extra food, but he couldn't free them.

On the afternoon of the fourth day, Mrs. Story begged the pirates to allow her whole family to be out in the fresh air and sunshine at the same time.

Reluctantly, the pirates agreed and gave them free run of the deck, but as the afternoon wore on, they started quarrelling about their plans for the evening. Theo was afraid the pirates might lock them all back in their cabin again. He had to do something! When all the men happened to be belowdecks, he told Nicole to get under the folds of the sail he had slept on.

"No matter what happens, stay here and don't move," he whispered. "I'm going to keep you free tonight. Shh! Here they come."

Red's bald head emerged from the hatch. "What I want to know is when we're going to get word back from Philadelphia?"

"Just keep ye sails set," urged Dr. Patch, who followed Red up on deck.

"Sails set! More'n likely, that tinker you gave those gold doubloons to headed south to Charlotte. If I ever see him again, it'll be to watch him walk the plank!"

"Now, why wouldn't he deliver our demands to the governor? These things take time, Red. The governor is probably workin' to get Cap'n back right now."

"Maybe," grumbled Red, "but in the meantime, I'm gonna sleep in a real bed tonight. I'm tired of that stinkin' hold. My hammock curls my back like a hermit crab in a too-small shell."

"None of ye's got overnight shore leave," declared Dr. Patch, spreading both hands as though calming troubled waters. He looked around at Cobo, who was just emerging from the hold. "We all return to the ship together, me hardies. It's all for one and one for all."

"Who made you captain?" said Cobo. "If it's one for all and all for one, then we *all* get beds tonight. Whaddya say, lads?"

"Hear! Hear!" chimed in Jerry from the hold.

Theo came and stood beside his mother as she leaned her elbows on the ship's railing and looked longingly at the north riverbank. "I've got Nicole hidden away in the sails," he whispered. "Maybe they'll get so worked up they'll forget to lock us away for the night."

His mother glanced back over her shoulder. "It's more likely that they'll lock us *all* away."

Theo studied the water between the ship and the north bank. It was much closer than the other side, not more than fifty feet. He could swim twice that far easily. Even Nicole could. If they could just stay out of the cabin, they definitely could get away from the ship! But then what?

All the pirates were back on deck. "Leavin' the ship unattended all night's foolish talk," snorted Patch. "Someone could discover the *Nighthawk*, and if we not be here to defend her, all could be lost."

Cobo rolled his eyes. "Who's going to find her in the middle of the night?" He pointed up into the rigging. "Take a climb up Jacob's ladder there and see for yourself. I told you, she's not visible even during the day."

Theo turned from the rail to watch the men. Cobo's eyes narrowed at the doctor. "Or are you *afraid* to go aloft?" He looked around at the other mates. "You know, in all the time I've known Doc, I've never seen him up in the riggin'. You don't think he could be yellow, now, do you?"

"It ain't me job to be monkeyin' around aloft. I be a doctor, and that takes all me skills."

"Uh-hum, some skill, but you couldn't save Joey! Besides, whaddya think it takes to keep from fallin' off those ropes when they're covered with ice and it's blowin' up a gale? That's skill, too!"

Cobo glared at Dr. Patch, and the silence tightened. Finally Patch muttered, "All the same, it'd be foolish to be away too long."

"Then *you* stay here and practice 'monkeyin' around up there,' as you call it," put in Red. "Me and the mates'll find nice warm beds."

"No, no. You swabbies be likely to run ye mouths in that tavern. If one of us goes, we all go."

"Sounds right to me," declared Cobo, and the argument was over.

In a few minutes they were all climbing down the rope ladder to the dinghy. Theo held his breath and looked at his mother. Maybe this was their chance! Maybe the pirates would leave them all free. He could hear the men finding their seats in the crowded little boat while trying not to tip it over.

Then, just when they thought their chance for freedom had come, Cobo popped back up over the side of the ship. "Mrs. Story, I almost forgot to see you 'home.' How ungentlemanly of me after you gave me that Bible and all. May I walk you to your door?"

He looked around. "And let's see, where's the girl?"

"Uh." Mrs. Story put her finger to her mouth as though she were trying to remember. Then she smiled broadly. "Why, I believe she went to lie down."

Cobo nodded and looked at Theo. "Seein' as how you folks haven't had anything to eat yet this evening, and I don't have any time to serve you, I guess we'll let the boy stay out again. You haven't minded sleepin' out, have you?"

Theo shook his head.

"That's what I thought. Kids always like a little adventure," he said with a wink to Mrs. Story. "Anyway, boy, you get something from the galley for your mother and sister, but don't mess with anything else."

Chapter 8

Treasure in the Hold

As soon as the pirates were out of sight, Theo pulled Nicole out from under the sail. She brushed herself off. "I thought I was going to die under there. Have they gone yet?"

"Yes, they've gone."

"Does that mean we're free?"

"*We* are, but Mama is not. Come on, let's go talk to her."

Through the grate of the cabin door, Mrs. Story encouraged the kids to not give up. "God will make a way. He hasn't brought us this far just to leave us." After a few moments of silence, she added, "At least tonight there are two of us free.

That's the best yet."

"Yeah, I guess so," said Theo. "But what you said earlier is true. They know that by keeping any one of us locked up, we are all held captive."

"Well, let's not brood over what we can't change. Why don't you two go get something for us to eat. I have no idea what you will find down there."

In the galley, Theo and Nicole found some corned beef preserved in a barrel of salt. They boiled a piece of it with some potatoes, onions, and carrots. "Now, this is a proper English dinner," grinned Nicole. "We should've been eating like this every night."

But getting the food to their mother through the grating on the door was not so easy. They actually had to feed her, one spoonful at a time. Before long, she had them all laughing over the strange process. As Nicole was finishing her turn, Theo wandered away. A molten sun was setting in its crimson bed of clouds, but the beauty did not interest Theo.

Before this whole experience of being a captive, he had imagined how exciting the life of a pirate might be—sailing the seven seas, hunting down galleons laden with gold, capturing treasure. But the life of these pirates was as boring as watching the shadow move on a sundial. They argued all day and drank all night. What good did their treasure do them?

Treasure. The treasure in the hold!

Theo poked his head around the corner of the gangway. "Nicole, I'm going below. If you hear anyone coming, warn me immediately. I don't want to get caught down there."

"How come?" she said. "Cobo said you could go down and get us some food. So why would he be angry if he found you there?"

"I don't have time to explain. Just do as I say, and keep a close lookout."

Theo hurried below and stumbled around until he lit the lantern, not worrying this time about being quiet. Theo opened the door in the bulkhead, stepped into the cargo hold, and held up the lamp. Even though he had been there just a couple days before, it was like exploring a familiar old cellar you hadn't visited for years. There were the bales and barrels and sea chests, right where they should be. And there was *the* chest.

He knelt down. Would the lock still be open? Yes. With trembling hands he removed it and slowly lifted the lid, almost afraid the chest would be full of nothing but dirty old rags that had fooled him on first glance.

But no. Brilliant treasure shone back at him— gold bars, dragoons, silver coins, small leather bags of gold dust, and all kinds of gem-studded jewelry. And there on the top was the pocket watch he had seen Dr. Patch steal from the captain of the *Loyal Tradesman*. Theo wanted to touch it all, to dig his hands deep into the cold metal and feel it flow through his fingers like cool sand, but something held him back as though if he touched it, it would burn his skin. Slowly he lowered the lid and replaced the lock.

An idea was coming to him.

Excited, but also frightened by the grandeur of the wealth, Theo climbed back up to the deck and went to the cabin, where he told his mother and sister about the treasure.

"Just think of what we could do with all that treasure," he concluded.

"But, Theo," said his mother, "what good will all that treasure do us if we're confined to this ship? The only thing we should care about is getting free. Besides, that gold is not ours."

"I know, I know. But you said that if I left, the pirates might sail away with you and Nicole—but they *wouldn't* sail away if they didn't have the treasure. If we got it into Tammany's canoe, we could go bury it somewhere. Then we could use it to buy our freedom," suggested Theo.

"What do you mean, 'buy our freedom'?"

"Well, they're trying to use us as ransom to free Captain Kidd, aren't they? Why can't we use the treasure as ransom to free *us*? Once I'm gone with the gold, you could tell them that I will return it only when they release you. Think about it, Mama. There's an awful lot of it, and they would never leave it behind."

"But how would we keep from getting recaptured? We have no means of getting to safety. If we started walking north, they could overtake us," said his mother. "I don't know. I don't think this will work."

Back and forth they went, discussing various options, until Tammany, silent as smoke from a cooking fire, drifted into the gangway behind Theo and Nicole.

"Tammany," said Mrs. Story, who saw him first, "thank you for coming."

Quickly they told him of their ideas—and their problems.

Tammany looked steadily at Mrs. Story for a few moments. "If you take the treasure, you should take it all the way to Governor Penn in Philadelphia. Then you would have protection."

"What? Philadelphia?" Theo shook his head. "No, you don't understand. This is *gold*, lots of gold. It is very, very heavy. Two men could barely lift the chest. It would take us several trips in your canoe just to get it off the ship. Even if you and Nicole and I carried all we could lift, that wouldn't even be half of it. And we could never haul it all the way to Philadelphia."

"Then we won't use my canoe to go back and forth to the riverbank. We'll use that boat tied behind the ship, go back to the bay, then sail it all the way up the Delaware River to Philadelphia."

The longboat? Everyone was silent as the plan blossomed in their minds. It just might work. The longboat had remained tied behind the ship ever since the pirates had used it to explore the river. Since they had found a shorter way to Dover Tavern by crossing the dunes, they had basically forgotten about it. But Theo and Nicole both knew how to sail. Their parents had taught them how to swim at a young age, and just a year before, they had taken sailing lessons in a small skiff on the river. Though larger, the longboat couldn't be that much more difficult to sail.

Nicole was the first to speak. "What do you think, Mama?"

"It might work, it might at that . . . if those pirates don't come back early."

By the light of the lantern, Theo and Nicole and Tammany stepped over the sill in the bulkhead and into the dark, musty hold. Theo led them to the chest, and Nicole reached down and drew her fingers across its rough top. "I want to see the treasure."

"Not now. We've got to get it out of here," said Theo.

"Why not? You got to see it. It will only take a minute." And before Theo could stop her, she removed the lock and lifted the lid. "Ohh!" she breathed.

"Don't touch . . ." But Nicole had already grabbed a handful of coins and was letting them clink back into the chest.

Slowly Theo reached down and picked up the watch. "This belonged to the captain of the *Loyal Tradesman*."

"The first ship we were on? How do you know?"

"Because I saw Patch steal it out of his pocket." He held it up to his ear. "It's still ticking. It must be a very fine watch to stay wound this long."

They all got quiet as he held it to Nicole's ear. But

what they heard was the faraway voice of Mrs. Story. "Theo! Nicole!" Their names drifted down the hatch and through the ship.

Eyes wide in fear, Nicole slammed the lid of the chest, put the lock through the hasp, and snapped it closed.

Theo sucked in his breath. "Oh no! You locked it!"

For an instant she gave him a "So what?" look, then turned and ran to the steps and climbed up through the hatch as Theo jammed the watch into his pocket.

"Do you think someone is coming?" Nicole asked as they all scrambled up to the deck.

"I don't know."

But when they arrived at their mother's door, she simply wanted to suggest that they pull the longboat up alongside the ship on the side opposite the rope ladder. "That way if the pirates come back early, they might not notice it."

Theo groaned. "Is that all you wanted?"

"Well, yes. But it's important."

"But you scared us silly calling us like that!"

Back in the hold, the chest proved to be heavier than they had imagined. All three of them dragged and struggled and pulled and lifted just to get it into position at the base of the hatch steps. Even in the damp, cool air, sweat dripped from their faces and down their backs.

"Those steps are too steep. We'll never get it up on deck," said Nicole.

Tammany and Theo stood looking up. The deck,

only seven feet above, seemed a mile away. Theo looked back down at the chest. "If you hadn't closed that lock, Nicole, we could take the treasure up bit by bit and load it into the longboat that way. Now we have to move the whole chest or nothing."

"We need rope," said Tammany, still looking up.

"Rope . . . yes . . . rope," agreed Theo, now also looking up through the hatch as though a plan was written in the stars above. "And . . . and a block and tackle. And we could build a crane from the boom for the sail and lower the chest directly into the longboat."

But the plan was not as easily carried out as described. Rope, block, and tackle were easy enough to find, but rigging a crane was another matter. It took hours to attach all the ropes, and then they discovered that the chest was still too heavy, even with a block and tackle. Hearing them struggle unsuccessfully, Mrs. Story called from her cabin, "Use the capstan!"

Theo relaxed his pull on the rope and looked over at the winch in the middle of the ship. Of course. That was exactly what it was for, to give increased power for raising the anchor or the sails or pulling in any other heavy line.

They quickly wrapped their rope around it and secured it, and then, as Nicole watched the chest down in the hatch, Theo and Tammany began to walk around the capstan, pushing on the handles. The block and tackle creaked and the line tightened.

"It's coming! It's coming!" said Nicole.

Finally the valuable chest was lowered onto the deck. After hours of effort, their plan was working.

"Hurry," said Tammany, pointing to the eastern horizon. It was just possible to detect an amber glow above the dunes.

"Yes," said Theo, "the pirates will be back soon."

To pull the longboat along the starboard side of the *Nighthawk* as Mrs. Story had suggested, Theo and Tammany had to cut the rope that ran from the stern of the ship to the cottonwood tree on shore. Otherwise the mast of the longboat would not pass under it. While they were doing this and getting the boat into position, Nicole raided the galley for some bread and cheese and flasks of water.

"Don't forget a blanket or two," called their mother.

When everything was ready, they skidded the chest over to the edge of the ship and then swung the boom out over the side. By this time, the sky was getting light enough that they didn't need the lantern to do their work. Nicole climbed down a rope into the boat.

"Guide it so it comes down right there in the center," said Theo. "But don't get under it. If something slipped, it could fall on you."

Again the capstan and the tackle strained as the chest rose from the deck and swung out over the longboat. Slowly it lowered into place, and the ropes went slack.

They'd done it.

But as Nicole climbed back up onto the *Nighthawk*, they heard voices.

The pirates were returning from Dover Tavern.

Chapter 9

Race for the Fog

B E CAREFUL . . . and don't forget the blankets," Mrs. Story whispered through the door's grate.

"Good-bye, Mama. We'll be back soon." Theo took Nicole's hand and bent over as they headed for the edge of the ship, hoping that the pirates wouldn't see them. Tammany was already waiting in the longboat, ready to cast off.

Nicole started to sit beside the chest and then stopped. "Your canoe. The pirates will see your canoe before they even get to the ship."

Tammany grabbed the rope and, hand-over-hand, walked up the side of the *Nighthawk* as easily as if he were on flat ground. Time passed. Why wasn't he back yet? All they could hear was the *squeak, squeak, squeak* of the oars in the pirates' dinghy on the other side of the ship. And then Tammany was there, sliding back down the rope and dropping into the longboat.

"I cut it loose and gave it a shove," he whispered as he untied the longboat and pushed off from the pirate ship with an oar.

They were on their way—and with the treasure chest, too.

The longboat drifted away from the ship several feet . . . then came to a stop in the water. The air was so still that the sail didn't even flutter, but why wasn't the current taking them downstream toward the bay? Were they hung up in some weeds? Had they grounded on an unseen sandbar?

"It's the tide," whispered Tammany. "It's coming in and blocks the river's current." He pointed to a little patch of foam on the water. It remained as still as they were.

Voices of the pirates came to them sharp and clear across the still water. "How come I always have to row this dinghy?" It sounded like Jerry.

" 'Cause that's all you're good for." That was Red.

"Theo!" Nicole whispered. "They're going to catch us!"

Theo grabbed the tiller and with a frown to Tammany, he nodded at the oars. Tammany picked them up and quietly placed them in the locks. "Don't let them splash," Theo whispered. Tammany shook his head and rowed as silently as a snake in the water.

By the time they came around the stern of the

Nighthawk, the dinghy was empty and the pirates were up on deck.

"Hey, where's that blasted kid? And what are all these ropes doing on deck?"

"Look, the boom's loose. Somebody's been jury-riggin' our ship."

Then Cobo appeared on the poop deck peering over the stern railing, and the kids heard the words they feared most: "They took the longboat! Hey, you, come back here!"

"Pull harder," Nicole urged Tammany, but by then all four pirates were yelling and cursing as they pointed across the water at them.

Theo had no idea how they acted so quickly, but in a minute or two the pirates had loaded one of the brass swivel guns on the back of the ship and were aiming it toward them. "Get down in the bottom of the boat!" he ordered Nicole, then moved up beside Tammany to take one of the oars.

His quick movement almost upset the longboat, but with no wind there was no reason to stay at the tiller, they might as well have the benefit of two people at the oars.

The cannon boomed, and the ball buzzed over them to plunge into the quiet water.

"Ye better turn back!" came a yell from Dr. Patch. "We don't yearn to hurt ye none, but ye dare not take our longboat."

"Do they know we have the chest?" Nicole asked anxiously.

"Let's hope not," grunted Theo, pulling his oar.

"It'd just make them all the more determined to get us."

"But if they knew we had their treasure chest," she said, peering fearfully back at the ship, "they wouldn't try to sink us. Tell them! They're getting ready to fire again!"

Theo and Tammany glanced at each other. Tammany nodded.

The boys stopped rowing and Theo yelled, "Don't shoot! We have the treasure chest!" He pointed to it. "If you sink this boat, you'll lose it, too."

There was immediate confusion and debate between the pirates on the ship, then Cobo disappeared—probably to check the hold. A moment later, all the pirates left the poop deck, and the boys pulled on their oars again.

Suddenly, Theo felt a chill. He was having trouble seeing the pirate ship. He was having trouble seeing anything. Was he getting sick? Was he going to pass out? It all happened so quickly that he didn't realize what was going on until Tammany brought him back to reality.

"Fog! We're saved by a morning fog."

None of them had seen it because all their attention had been on the pirate ship behind them and the possibility that they would soon be sunk. Gratefully they took a break from rowing as the fog's clammy fingers enfolded them.

Mother must have been praying very hard.

After a brief rest, Theo said, "Let's row to the bank."

"Why?"

"I gotta go back. I've been thinking. We've got to disable the ship. If we don't, they'll follow us. The fog's going to burn off soon, and then a breeze will come up. It may take them some time to turn the ship around and maneuver it down the river, but once they do, the *Nighthawk* can sail much faster than we can. They would be likely to catch us by the middle of the afternoon, or before."

"What are you going to do?" asked Nicole, her face puckered with worry.

"I don't know. Disable the rudder, cut the sails, something."

Tammany picked up the oars and turned the boat toward shore. Soon they were rewarded by the crunch of the bow on the sand. Theo tore off his jacket and dropped it into the boat. Then he jumped out and pulled the boat in a little. "Wait here. I'll be back soon."

"Theo! Be careful!" Nicole cried after him as Theo took off at a trot.

He climbed two or three dunes so soft he slid back one step for every two he took forward, and at one point had to wade through a swamp up to his waist. But soon he had traveled upriver far enough to emerge from the fog and could see the *Nighthawk* only a short distance ahead.

As he approached cautiously, his confidence sagged. What, exactly, could he do to disable the ship? Then he saw all four pirates cramped in the little dinghy, rowing downstream after the longboat.

Good. He wouldn't have to contend with them on board the *Nighthawk* . . . but he'd have to hurry so he could get back to the longboat before the pirates found them.

As he came to the edge of the water, he noticed that the ship's stern had drifted farther from the shore. Then he realized why: He and Tammany had cut the rope between it and the cottonwood tree so they could move the longboat up alongside the ship.

That's what he would do. He would set the ship completely adrift. As soon as the tide went out, it would move downriver until it hit a sandbar. Without a team of oxen or an exceptionally high tide, it would be stuck there for days, maybe weeks. Not only would the pirates be unable to chase them, but they wouldn't be able to escape with his mother, even if they were willing to give up their treasure.

He had them now!

Twenty minutes later he was back at the longboat, panting so hard he thought he was going to drop.

"Theo!" cried Nicole. "What . . . what did you do?"

"I cut it . . . adrift. . . . It'll ground itself . . . on a sandbar," he panted, pushing them off from shore.

Tammany pulled hard on the oars, but even though the fog was already starting to thin, he stayed close to the north bank so that he could be certain of going in the right direction. Then he stopped and put a finger to his lips and then his hand to his ear.

Theo strained to listen.

Creak, creak, creak. It was the noisy oar on the pirates' dinghy, but which direction were they? He held both hands to his ears and turned his head. Then he pointed.

Tammany shook his head and pointed in another direction. Nicole nodded her head vigorously and pointed in the same direction. It was strange how the fog could play tricks.

Slowly Tammany began rowing again, taking extra care to avoid noise. They could tell that they were slightly ahead of the pirates, but it was not by much, and the pirates were keeping pace with them.

As soon as Theo got his breath back, he gestured to Tammany that he wanted to come up and help him row. Maybe with two of them rowing again, they could outrun the pirates. But as he changed position, the oar clattered to the bottom of the boat, creating a sound as distinct as a buoy bell in the fog.

"Over there!" came a shout out of the mist. "I see a shadow—it's them!"

Suddenly a pistol fired, and a ball whizzed through the air. "Stop and we won't harm you!" yelled Patch. "We only want what's ours."

Theo and Tammany rowed harder.

O Lord, let the fog get denser.

"I say stop now! . . . We'll let you go if you return our chest. . . . You can have the dinghy, and we'll take the longboat. Now, you gotta admit that's more than a fair trade since neither one of the boats belonged to you in the first place!"

Theo looked at his sister and saw the questions in her wide, frightened eyes. But would the pirates release their mother? And how would they get back to Philadelphia in a dinghy? He saw Nicole give a slight shake of her head. No, they couldn't trust Patch.

Theo pulled harder, and soon the fog swallowed them again.

Chapter 10

Humming in the Wind

THEY COULD STILL HEAR the *creak, creak, creak* of the dinghy oar. Then Theo realized that he and Tammany were rowing so hard that *their* oars sometimes splashed in the water, creating noise that the pirates could follow. But did they dare slow down?

Suddenly, Nicole tapped Theo on the knee and pointed to the north where they had been keeping the bank in sight so they wouldn't get lost in the fog. But the bank wasn't there!

Theo looked at the water around them. There were no waves, but then the morning was very calm. The water was still brownish, but maybe it would turn blue farther out. He nudged Tammany. "I think we're in the bay," he mouthed.

111

Tammany nodded and pointed north, so they swung the longboat in that direction and continued to row but more quietly than before. A sea gull cried and swooped low over them as it disappeared into the silent fog.

Silence. Even the creaking of the dinghy oar was gone. Had they escaped the pirates? Or had their cunning enemies wrapped a rag around the oar to quell the sound, realizing that it gave away their position? Theo touched Tammany's arm, and they both stopped rowing to listen. There was no sound except the quiet lapping of water along the shore.

Beside them a small limb from a sunken tree poked out of the water. The longboat drifted to a stop beside it, and Theo absentmindedly reached out for it, but the limb seemed to move away. Not only had the longboat stopped its forward motion, it was now going backward. "Look, we're in a current!" he whispered.

"The tide has turned," whispered Tammany.

Theo looked around. The fog was starting to break up, and to their port side he could see the dim shadows of the shore. But to his shock, he also saw land to their starboard. "Look! We're not in the bay. This is still the river, but we're going up it."

Tammany looked from shore to shore. "No, no. We've turned up another river by mistake. This is part of Bombay Hook. All these rivers are a tangled mess around here. I should have known."

Theo was silent for a few moments as he tried to make out things on land. Finally he said, "But if the tide has turned, then all we have to do is float downstream with the current, and it will soon spit us out into the bay. Right?" He had forgotten to whisper, though he had kept his voice very low.

Tammany hesitated. "Yes. I guess that might work." He peered through the mist at the banks on either side of the river as Theo pulled on his oar to turn the boat around until it pointed downstream. Here the riverbanks were no longer steep and eroded by the river, but low and gentle, not much more than sandbars rising out of the water.

Theo looked up. The fog was breaking apart. He could see a patch of blue sky as a breeze swirled through the mists. He glanced behind them at the limb sticking out of the water that had shown him that they were in a current. It was already twenty yards back up the river. They were moving rapidly. Then he noticed a worried look on Tammany's face. "What's the matter?"

"We're drifting right toward the pirates."

The Indian boy was right. What would happen when the fog no longer hid them?

The breeze came stronger. "Let's put up the sail," Theo said. "We might get some help from the wind, and if we're going fast enough, we might zip past them."

While Nicole scanned the water ahead and Tammany kept the oars in hand, Theo raised the sail. A puff of wind caught the sail and almost tipped them over before Theo released the mainsheet. Nicole fell to the bottom of the boat, and Tammany dropped his oars with a clatter. Nicole gave Theo a dirty look. "Be careful!"

He shrugged and gave her a look that said, "I'm sorry," but she continued to glare at him as though he had intended to knock her over. He got situated at the back of the boat, holding the tiller with one hand and the mainsheet with the other. The breeze wasn't steady, but the puffs that filled the sail and caused the boat to heel over came every few moments and moved them faster than the current.

Staring ahead into the grayness, Theo watched as the fog suddenly lifted from the water like a curtain on a stage, and there, crammed in the little dinghy like four men in a tub, were the pirates.

"There they be!" came Patch's voice across the water. "After 'em, mates."

"We got 'em now," chimed in Red, pulling hard on the oars.

"Turn back, turn back," urged Tammany.

Theo hesitated. "But . . . but this is a river. There's no way out."

"Well, we sure can't get past them. Look, if they don't sink us, they're going to kill us."

Indeed, Dr. Patch was aiming his pistol right at them. But just as he pulled the trigger, Cobo knocked the barrel to the side. Smoke puffed from the end, accompanied by a loud crack.

Theo wasted no more time attempting to figure a better escape route. He brought the longboat around as sharply as he could. Several seconds passed as they lost speed. Then the sail caught a fresh breeze,

and the little craft leaned over and began to move upstream.

"Row, Tammany! You too, Nicole."

Nicole moved into the seat by Tammany, and they both began pulling on the oars to add to the power of the sail. Slowly the distance between them and the pirates increased.

"Will they hurt Cobo?" asked Nicole as the pirates' angry shouts came to them over the water.

Theo glanced back over his shoulder. "Not Cobo. He'll be fine."

But would *they* be fine? Where were they going? How would they escape?

Twenty minutes later, the pirates were so far behind that their quarreling was no louder than the buzz of a fly caught in a cobweb. Tammany and Nicole stopped rowing and let the sail do the work. The breeze was strong enough now that the small waves slapped gently against the bow of the boat.

"Theo!" Tammany shaded his eyes with his hand against the glare of the sun as he looked toward the east. "Look to the starboard. I think there might be a second outlet to the bay."

Theo turned the boat in that direction as much as the wind would allow, and the closer they got to that side of the river, the more it looked like there was, indeed, a second small stream that flowed from the river across the sand and into the bay. If so, they had actually been sailing past an island.

"Come on," said Nicole. "Let's go over there."

"I can't turn into the wind any sharper. The sail is already starting to flap. Use the oars."

Nicole and Tammany pulled on the oars while Theo steered until they were in a shallow stream flowing across the wide, sandy beach. But it was flowing toward the bay. In fact, now they could actually see the bay, its wide silver surface shimmering in a sun made white by the morning's hazy sky.

Then the keel along the bottom of the longboat

scraped into the sandy bottom of the small stream and they came to a halt.

Theo jumped out. "Come on. Help me! Let's push it across. We can do it."

Tammany climbed out, too. The water came halfway up his calves. But he did not start pushing. Instead, he sloshed on down the stream.

"Where are you going?"

"To see if we really *can* get through. We don't want to get the boat so stuck in here that we can't get out." He waded down the stream until he came to the edge of the bay; then he ran back. "I think we can do it. It's worth a try."

Nicole climbed out, even though the bottom of her skirts got soaked, and together all three began pushing on the boat. Without their weight, it floated higher and free of the sand, and soon they were maneuvering it over a buried driftwood log and around a shallow spot until it was floating freely in the waters of Delaware Bay.

By noon the shores on either side of the bay were nothing more than narrow strips of land to the east and to the west. The three young mariners were in the middle of the bay, with a good breeze filling their sail, and there was not a pirate in sight.

"I wonder how long those pirates tried to follow us up that river," said Nicole, who was taking her turn at the tiller.

Theo opened his eyes and raised his head from the seat where he was resting after a sleepless night of hard work. "Probably quite a while if they didn't see that little outlet we took."

Tammany, who was lying in the prow of the boat, said, "I think I know what river we were on back there. It snakes around and comes back on itself a dozen times. They could travel up it all day and not be more than a mile from the *Nighthawk* by land."

Theo sat up. "I wonder what happened to the ship."

"I wonder what happened to Mama. Do you think she's safe, Theo?"

"Of course she's safe. The worst thing that could've happened is that the *Nighthawk* might have listed over a little when it went aground on one of those sandbars." Then he added, "I'd sure love to see the looks on the faces of those pirates when they come back to find their ship aground." He laughed aloud.

They were all enjoying the afternoon on the water. Tammany shifted his position, "When I was a little boy, our village was near a river, but through the middle of the village ran a stream. We kids would have contests. We would each put a leaf in the stream above the village and then follow it down to see whose leaf would go farthest before it got caught on a rock or in some grass or sank in a whirlpool. The rule was that we couldn't use anything but a leaf, and we couldn't touch it." He paused for a moment. "But sometimes we did blow on them to keep them away from the bank. That wasn't really cheating."

"How far did they go?" asked Nicole.

"Usually not very far." Tammany laughed nervously. "Sometimes one of the dogs would see us playing and try to join in. He would wade right into the stream and grab the leaf with his mouth. Boy, that made us mad. But you know, one time my leaf made it all the way to the river, and I was the big winner."

Theo waited for Tammany to continue. He had such a worried look on his face, as though his story had some tragic ending, but his leaf had won. What more was there to tell?

"Theo," Nicole spoke up, "do you think the pirates will get back in time to fix Mother her dinner?"

He looked at Nicole, trying to recall her question. "Well, sure," he said, trying to sound confident. "They'll be getting hungry themselves. Besides, even if they're late, she still had some water and leftover bread in the cabin. Say, speaking of food, where's the cheese and bread you brought for us?"

Nicole made no move to get the bag on the bottom of the boat. "But what if the pirates are so angry at you cutting their ship loose that they won't feed her?"

"Cobo won't let that happen."

He dug into the bag with their food and broke off pieces for Tammany, Nicole, and himself. Then he passed around the water flask. It was actually getting hot beneath the bright sun.

After they had eaten, Theo took another turn at the tiller while Nicole and Tammany fell asleep.

Theo had offered, but it did not seem that Tammany was interested in learning how to sail. Maybe that was for the best; this was no time or place for an accident.

He looked up at the sun, trying to figure what time it was, and then he grabbed his jacket that was lying in the bottom of the boat and felt the pocket, remembering the captain's watch he had put there. He pulled it out and examined it. On the back was an engraving that he had not noticed before, which read, "Thanks for being your 'sister's keeper' when it mattered most. Ever grateful, Isabelle."

Theo looked out over the water. What could it mean? He remembered how he had used the phrase from the Bible about not being his brother's keeper after Bernie Bevan was injured in the cannon blast. When he had looked up the verse, he had decided Governor Penn was right: He should have been his brother's keeper. There had been something he could have done that might have prevented Bernie's death.

And yet, back on the *Loyal Tradesman*, he had again decided not to speak up when he knew something wrong was happening. He had excused his silence, telling himself he had merely observed the theft of the captain's watch and it wasn't his business. But, as with Bernie, the ultimate consequences were far more serious. His silence had led to his family being taken hostage by pirates.

He looked at the engraving again. Apparently, the captain had taken care of his sister, maybe looked out for her at some point when he could have looked the other way. Theo looked at his own sister sleeping in the bottom of the boat. She could be a pest some-times . . . but he wanted to look out for her, and not only for her and his mother, but for anyone.

Theo set his jaw in determination and put the watch back in his jacket pocket. Never again would he see something wrong and keep silent simply for his own convenience. If Governor Penn approved, they would trade the chest of treasure for his mother's freedom. No one might know who the rightful own-ers were of all that treasure, but he sure knew to whom the pocket watch belonged. He would *make* it his business to return it to the captain of the *Loyal Tradesman*. It would be his way of sealing his deci-sion to be his "brother's keeper" from here on out.

He took a deep breath and pulled the sail's mainsheet tighter. In response, the longboat heeled over a little farther and picked up more speed so that the shroud lines began to hum in the wind.

Chapter 11

Capsized

B<small>Y EVENING THE YOUNG SAILORS</small> were well up into the Delaware River. Aside from a few houses along the shore, they had seen no one. And they feared stopping at any of those houses because of the treasure chest they carried and the chance that it might be stolen if the settler wasn't honest.

Finally they pulled the longboat into a deserted section of shore along the eastern bank of the river and began to set up for the night.

"If we had seen an Indian camp, we could have stopped there," said Tammany as he 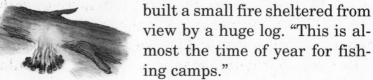 built a small fire sheltered from view by a huge log. "This is almost the time of year for fishing camps."

"But," said Nicole, "if we're afraid that some settlers might steal the treasure, how could we be sure that Indians wouldn't take it, especially if we didn't know them?"

Theo snorted. "What would Indians do with a whole chest of gold and silver? It's not even their kind of money. They use wampum."

"Oh, we would know what to do with it." Tammany raised up from where he had been blowing on the sparks he had knocked into the tinder with his steal and flint. He gave Theo a hard look. "We would know what to do with it. Don't ever doubt that. But there are other reasons we would not take your precious treasure."

Theo let it rest for the time, but after they had eaten and were each rolled in their blankets round the glowing embers, he said, "Tell me, Tammany, how can you be so sure that no Indian would take the treasure?"

Tammany was silent for so long that Theo wondered if he had offended him, but finally he answered. "It is because of William Penn. He does not take our land as other whites have. He asks us and then pays us a fair price." Tammany fell silent again. Theo thought he would say no more, but then the Indian boy continued.

"Many years ago, before I was born, at the council of Shakamaxon, where the great Indian kings gathered, William Penn said words that all Iroquois and Shawnees remember and pass on. They were these: 'The Great Spirit who made me and you, who rules the heavens and earth, and who knows the innermost thoughts of men, knows that I and my friends have a hearty desire to live in peace and friendship with you, and to serve you to the utmost of our power. . . . I will consider you as the same flesh and blood with the Christians, and the same as if one man's body were to be divided into two parts.'"

Tammany stirred up the glowing embers. "He has been true to those words ever since, breaking no treaties and doing no harm. That treasure chest in the boat is Governor Penn's business. And to us he is more than a brother. We are one, and one would not steal from himself."

Theo remained respectfully silent in case Tammany had more to say, but the Indian boy pulled his blanket up over his head and adjusted his position for sleep.

After a moment, Theo rolled onto his back and stared at the field of stars across the moonless sky. Why were the Indians so ready to respect William Penn while so many colonists claimed the liberty to do what was wrong? Where was their sense of community and responsibility—owning slaves, refusing to pay taxes to support the government, looking the other way when pirates brought them profits? It was all so irresponsible, so selfish . . . not unlike how he had acted concerning the cannon and the pocket watch.

But all that was going to change for him.

They got an early start the next morning, but it did them no good. What little wind there was blew down the river toward the sea. They had to tack back and forth, working against the current and the wind. Finally Tammany said, "I think we would make more progress rowing." So he and Theo took the oars while Nicole held the tiller to keep their course.

"I wish I knew how Mama was," Nicole worried. "I don't like leaving her alone on that ship. What if those pirates sail off to Cuba or Jamaica with her?"

Theo skipped a beat in his rowing and patted the treasure chest in front of him. "Don't forget this. They're not going anyplace without this, so don't worry."

"But what if they do? What if they decide that their freedom is worth more than all that gold?"

Theo resumed pulling on his oar. "Huh? If they believed that, they wouldn't have stolen it in the first place."

"Not necessarily," put in Tammany. "Governor Penn says that it is only the fear of God, who knows all things, that turns the heart from evil. They just didn't expect to get caught. No one expects to get caught doing wrong."

"But since we escaped, now they know they're going to get caught if they stay there, so they'll have to run, don't you think, Theo?"

Why did Nicole insist on worrying? "You forget, I set the *Nighthawk* adrift. It's stuck right now on some sandbar in Dona's River. It will take some mighty effort to get it free."

Nicole sighed. "I hope you're right."

That afternoon the wind began to change. First it came from the east, which made for good sailing, but then it swung around to the south, and they had the wind at their backs. They nearly flew up the Delaware River. As the longboat plowed ahead, spray from the waves cooled the young people. They were getting closer to home . . . and help.

Theo was at the tiller, and the sail was far out to the port side of the boat catching as much wind as possible, when Tammany announced from the front of the boat that the town of Philadelphia was in sight. Theo held his course until they were even with the newly built docks; then he pushed the tiller hard over to head in to shore.

But he turned too fast. The boat swung around until the wind caught the backside of the sail. Before Theo could pull in the mainsheet, the boom swung across, nearly hitting him and Nicole. He had jibed, and before he and Nicole could reposition their weight in the boat, the boat heeled over to a dangerous angle.

Both Theo and Nicole tried to scramble to the high side, but they were too late. The heavy treasure chest slid to the low side. Maybe another gust of wind added to their crisis . . . Theo never knew, because the next moment he was under the chilly water, pawing for the surface.

He broke into the air, gasping for breath, and immediately began looking around for Nicole and Tammany. Tammany popped up a moment later,

and Theo quickly saw that he could swim—*but where was Nicole?*

The capsized sailboat was bottom up just a few feet away. "Nicole! Nicole!" he shouted.

"Maybe she's on the other side," Tammany said

and immediately began to swim around the capsized longboat.

Theo didn't wait for good news. He dove underwater immediately. With Nicole's cumbersome skirts, she would have trouble swimming. Even Theo wished he could kick off his shoes and get out of his jacket, but there was no time for that. He looked down into the frigid darkness and saw a stream of bubbles rising from the depths, but there was no way he could go deeper without another breath.

He burst to the surface and was about to plunge below again when Tammany shouted, "Here! Here! She's over here! She's underneath the boat."

Theo treaded water and looked toward Tammany, who was hanging on to the side of the longboat and pointing under it. With hope, Theo swam to his side.

"She's in the boat."

Theo didn't understand, but he ducked under to have a look, and there was Nicole, at least her body and all her skirts. Her head was up inside the overturned boat. Theo eased himself up beside her and found that he emerged into the pocket of air captured inside the overturned hull of the boat.

"Nicole, are you all right?" It was so dark that he could barely see her outline.

"I'm scared, Theo. I don't want to let go." She was hanging on to the cross seat to keep her head well above the water.

"Yes, but you have to! We must get to shore. We're already drifting downstream with the current."

"But, Theo, these skirts. I'll never be able to swim in them. They'll drag me down."

"We'll help you. Tammany can swim, too. He's right outside the boat. Let's go."

They both dropped down into the cold water and came up out in the river. Tammany quickly came to their side, and together all three pulled for the shore. But the cold water was getting to them, and if some observant citizens hadn't been quick to throw them ropes, they might not have made it.

Soon the three young people were on the dock, shivering and dripping all over . . . but safe.

The treasure chest, however, was somewhere on the bottom of the Delaware River, probably still leaking a small stream of bubbles.

Chapter 12

The Phantom Ship

THE TWO MEN STOOD in the doorway, not wanting to dirty Governor Penn's slate-roofed house on Second Street where Theo, Nicole, and Tammany had been brought. The men were dirty, and both held their hats in their hands. "We are sorry, Governor, but we did not find the chest. We dragged the river where we thought the boat capsized, but we couldn't find a thing."

"Well, it doesn't matter now." The governor turned to Thomas Story, who was standing in the vestibule

with his arms around his children. "I'm not willing to negotiate with pirates anyway. We'll get your wife back, Thomas. You can count on that!"

130

Tammany had helped pinpoint the *Nighthawk*'s location on a map. The governor had quickly put together a plan. Thomas Story would travel on horseback with Colonel Robert Quary and a contingent of men down through Chester and New Castle and on south. Meanwhile, the governor would sail down the Delaware on the British navel sloop the *Phoenix*. The two forces would converge at Bombay Hook, trapping the pirates and rescuing Abigail Story.

"Tammany, I would like you to go with the overland posse as a guide. And, Theo"—the governor looked at Thomas Story as if for permission—"would you be willing to come with us on the *Phoenix*? We, also, might need someone who knows the exact location of the ship."

"Yes, sir."

"What about me?" Nicole demanded. "I want to go get Mama."

Mr. Story looked questioningly at the governor until he responded. "We should be safe on the *Phoenix*. Even though it's small, it's a well-armed vessel, and I'll personally look out for her."

The overland posse left before dark. The *Phoenix* got underway at dawn the next morning.

As the *Phoenix* emerged into Delaware Bay, the governor came up to stand beside Theo in the bow of the ship. Penn spoke casually, almost as though Theo weren't there.

"Before I left England, the king told me to make some new laws and enforce them. He even wanted me to establish a militia. I hate to do that, but I suppose we do need to do something." He sighed. "I would like to believe that if everyone followed the light within, we could live together in peace. But the Bible is right: 'There is a way which seemeth right unto a man, but the end thereof are the ways of death.' The only true Light is Jesus Christ . . . we cannot be a light to ourselves."

Theo said nothing but followed the governor's gaze as he looked off toward the eastern horizon where Cape May separated the Delaware Bay from the Atlantic Ocean.

"If people reject the Light of Christ to guide them from within, then they must live by laws from without, and to have any meaning, those laws must be enforced." Governor Penn slapped the railing. "Even if I don't raise a militia, I suppose I could set up some kind of a watch at the mouth of Delaware Bay to keep pirates out. But that's only part of the problem. A lot of 'good, honest people' are trading with these pirates and not reporting their evil deeds! Everybody just wants to live and let live, but let me tell you, son, society breaks down when we don't take responsibility for one another."

Theo thought about Bernie and the cannon and Dr. Patch stealing the captain's watch. He knew the governor was right. If someone else's "business" is to do wrong, you need to make it your business to stop them.

That night they anchored outside Bombay Hook, ready to go up the Dona's River the next morning and capture the *Nighthawk*. Hopefully the posse would be in position.

The next morning there was great excitement as the *Phoenix* hoisted its anchor. Again, there was no morning wind, so oars were extended and the sloop crept up the channel. On deck, Theo pointed out to the captain and the governor various landmarks he recognized. There weren't many. One dune looked pretty much like the next.

An hour passed, and they still hadn't found the *Nighthawk* stuck on a sandbar, tipping slightly over, as Theo had envisioned it. "But just up ahead," he assured them, "there's a sharp bend in the river. Not far beyond it we'll find a big cottonwood tree on the right where we tied up."

But when they came around the bend and were in sight of the gnarled old tree, all they found was Tammany, Thomas Story, and Colonel Quay standing on the bank with the other posse members and their horses.

The *Nighthawk* was gone!

"Where is this phantom ship that's supposed to be caught in this river?" called Colonel Quay from the bank.

"Maybe we have the wrong river!" yelled William Penn.

"No, no!" Theo pointed to the cottonwood tree. "Look there at the base of the tree. See, there's the rope I cut."

Thomas Story and Tammany ran over to the tree and began pulling in the line. When they got to the end, they held it up for everyone to see that it had been cut recently. "Looks like this was the place," called Story. "Do you think the pirates got to it and sailed away?"

"If they did," said the captain of the *Phoenix*, "they've got two to three days on us."

Maybe the pirates had sailed away in the ship, but a far worse possibility twisted Theo's stomach. He gulped and looked toward Tammany. The story about the leaf race. Had the Indian boy feared that the ship—like his leaf—might float all the way to open water? Theo didn't want to consider it!

"Colonel Quay," ordered the governor, "take some of your men and ride to that tavern, Dover Tavern, and see what they know about these pirates. And don't accept 'nothing' for an answer! People need to take some responsibility around here."

The colonel and his men returned an hour and a half later. Theo's heart leaped when he saw they had Dr. Patch and two of the other pirates in tow.

On the deck of the *Phoenix*, with their hands tied behind them, the pirates swore that when they got back with the dinghy, the ship was gone. "It be a phantom ship, Your Honor," said Patch, looking as sorrowful as he could.

"It was gone, just gone." Red and Jerry nodded

their agreement.

"Well, where's your dinghy, then?"

"Oh, Your Honor, that scoundrel Cobo stole it. We fired several shots at him, and Jerry, here, winged him. We could see the blood on the back of his shirt, but he kept on going down the river. He's probably drowned in the bay by now."

They shot Cobo? Theo looked anxiously down the river toward the bay. That's probably where his mother was, too. He couldn't believe that a ship the size of the *Nighthawk* could float down the river and out into the bay without going aground on a sandbar—but apparently it had. But they hadn't seen it in the bay. Could it . . . did that mean it had drifted on out into the open sea?

Two hours later the *Phoenix* was under full sail, racing toward the mouth of Delaware Bay with a watchman up in the crow's nest. But there was still no sight of the *Nighthawk*. Colonel Quay had been sent back to Philadelphia with the posse and the horses, while Thomas Story had come aboard the search ship. Everyone knew they had to find Mrs. Story soon or she might die of thirst or starvation locked in that cabin on board an empty ship.

"Captain, which way would the *Nighthawk* drift if she got out to sea?"

"Hard to say, Governor. The Gulf Stream would take her north if she got out into it, but yesterday and today there's been a contrary wind blowing south."

"Then let's look south first," said Mr. Story.

"Now, I'm not promising anything," said the captain, but he gave orders to change course to swing around Cape Henlopen and head south.

But as soon as they started to feel the swell of the open sea, the sailor aloft sang out, "Captain! I think we better go check that little harbor on the other side of Cape Henlopen. I can see the mast of a pretty good-sized ship in there, but it looks like it is lying partially over on its side. Maybe somebody careened it."

The *Phoenix* headed for the small harbor, and though they worried that it was a waste of time, they couldn't overlook any possibility.

Hidden by dunes, they couldn't see into the harbor until they made their last turn and headed into the channel. And there ahead, on the other side of the natural harbor, lay the *Nighthawk*, beached on her port side.

With all speed, the *Phoenix* anchored as close to shore as possible. Theo and Nicole joined their father and the governor and the captain in the hastily lowered longboat.

"Ahoy the *Nighthawk*!" the captain called as they approached the derelict ship. "Is anyone aboard?"

Theo searched the stern windows of the cabin where his mother had been held captive. "O Lord, let her be safe." But no handkerchief was waved from the window. No welcome voice called out.

Then the captain called out to a couple small children running along the beach just north of the ship. "Did you children see anyone aboard this ship?"

"Yes, sir," a boy of about eight called back. "They took 'em into town."

The sailors began rowing with all their strength for the few waterfront buildings that made up the town of Henlopen. As the longboat beached, Mr. Story took off running toward the houses, calling, "Abigail! Abigail!" while Theo and Nicole followed along behind.

The most welcome sound Theo had ever heard came from the porch of a small, neat house with a yard sign that said, *The Reverend Arthur Bannon.* "Over here, Thomas! Over here." There stood their mother, looking fine in a fresh white dress with a matching bonnet on her head.

"Mama! Mama!" screeched Nicole. Tears of joy flowed freely as the family united.

Finally Governor Penn asked the question that was in the back of everyone's mind. "Now, do tell us, Mrs. Story, how did you ever manage to guide that derelict ship into this small harbor when you were locked in the cabin, as I understand it? Was it an outright miracle of God?"

Abigail Story wiped her eyes and blew her nose, then said, "It was indeed a miracle, Governor, but not an accident. It was that pirate—I mean that sailor, Cobo—who saved my life.

"The ship floated down the river, just as Theo intended, bumping along the bottom, but it never

completely went aground on a sandbar. I was terri-
fied when I realized that we were bobbing around
out in the bay and I couldn't see any riverbanks out
the windows. At first I was most afraid that a storm
would come up and the *Nighthawk* would be ship-
wrecked on some rocky shore and I would drown.
But then hunger reminded me that there were other
ways to die.

"That night, or maybe it was early the next morning, I started hearing sounds on the deck. At first I thought I was losing my mind, but when there was enough light, I looked out the grating on the door and saw Cobo crawling up the gangway with a key in his hand. He was wounded and had lost so much blood that he could barely move and struggled for several minutes just to reach up and unlock my door.

"Well, I spent all that day and the following night nursing him while we floated around in . . . Delaware Bay, I guess. The next morning we had recovered enough for him to try to sail the ship. We were way out to sea by then. There was no land in sight. He took the wheel and instructed me in how to get a couple of the smaller sails up."

"Did you go aloft, Mama?" Nicole asked, eyes wide.

"Oh no! Just two of the smaller sails, barely enough to give us a little headway, but Cobo figured out where we were and guided us into Henlopen Harbor."

Theo glanced back down the short street toward the harbor. "Why did he beach it?"

Mrs. Story chuckled. "Well, it seems *somebody* had cut the anchor loose. There wasn't much else we could do. Besides, Cobo was so weak from a day's sailing that he completely collapsed as soon as we hit ground."

"How did he get on board in the first place?" asked Governor Penn.

"Apparently there had been an argument with

his . . . with the pirates. He chose to come after me, knowing that I would die without help. They shot him, but he came to my rescue anyway. Even as wounded as he was, he must have rowed that little dinghy all night before he caught up to me. I . . . wouldn't have made it without him."

Mr. Story cleared his throat and put his arm around his wife. "Where is this Cobo now? I think that I owe him my thanks, even if he is a pirate."

"They tell me that he died this morning," said Mrs. Story, tears coming again to her eyes. "But he sent me this." She held up a small gold cross that hung from a chain around her neck. "He saved my life."

Some time later, while the adults were thanking the people of Henlopen and preparing to return to the *Phoenix*, Theo and Nicole took a walk down on the beach to look at the *Nighthawk*.

"You know," said Nicole slowly, "I kind of liked Cobo."

"Me too." Theo pulled the watch out of his pocket and looked again at the inscription on the back: "Thanks for being your 'sister's keeper' when it mattered most. Ever grateful, Isabelle."

He thought about the New Testament Cobo had been reading. Maybe it *was* possible to really change . . . with the Light of Christ, that is.

More About Governor William Penn

WILLIAM PENN WAS BORN in London in 1644. He grew up there and in Ireland with all the privileges of the eldest son of Admiral Sir William Penn, who had captured Jamaica from the Dutch in 1655. Though very worldly as a youth, he became a Quaker in 1666 while a student at Oxford—very much to his father's disapproval. In 1668 Penn was arrested for writing a tract attacking the doctrines of the Church of England. While in prison in 1669, he wrote the devotional classic *No Cross, No Crown*. In spite of his father's disappointment in him, the admiral was finally able to arrange for William's release from prison.

After his father died in 1670, William began to feel that Quakers had no future in England and traveled to America in 1677 and 1678, looking for a safe haven. Then in 1681, as a settlement for a large debt owed to his father, William received "Pennsylvania" from King Charles II. Largely at his own expense, he financed a new colony as a home for Quakers and any other persecuted people. There Penn began his "Holy Experiment" of equal opportunity (he arranged for even poor people to earn a new home), religious tolerance, and fair and just treatment of the Indians. While massacres were commonplace in all the other American colonies, no white person was killed by an Indian during Penn's administration. His treaties with the Indians were the only ones never broken. Though the king had given Pennsylvania to him, Penn recognized the Indians as its rightful owners, and white people settled on it only with the permission of the Indians and after purchasing land from them. As a result, the Indians loved and honored Penn.

However, he himself experienced serious personal difficulties during the rest of his life. He was able to remain in his colony for only two brief periods (1682–1684, 1699–1701). He was twice accused of treason and lost control of Pennsylvania from 1692 to 1694 because of his friendship with the deposed English king, James II. His wife, Gulielma, died in 1694, and his eldest son, possibly spoiled by his father's lack of adequate discipline, became a disappointing rascal. Penn's financial reverses even landed him in debtors' prison briefly. When in 1699 he finally returned to Pennsylvania with his twenty-one-year-old daughter, Latitia, and his new wife, Hannah, he faced complications stemming from the extraordinarily tolerant policies on which he had founded his "Holy Experiment." Selfish-minded people were taking advantage of his relatively weak central government and generous policies.

To his dismay, he discovered that he "owned" three African slaves who worked his gardens at Pennsbury Manor (an estate manager ran his estate in his absence). He freed those slaves and did his best to get the government to end the slave trade and pass a law freeing all slaves after fourteen years of service, but the Assembly threw out his initiatives. The prevailing libertarian philosophy justified people doing as they pleased. (It was not until 1780 that the Society of Friends as a whole took a stand against slave holding.)

Pirates had also found Delaware Bay a haven for their operations. One explanation blamed Penn's own Quakers. Uncomfortable with using force to defend themselves, they were accused of accommodating the pirates and even profiting by trading with them. In some instances this represented a "live and let live" attitude gone to seed.

In this environment, rival factions flourished in the colony, making it difficult to agree, govern, or enforce laws or regulations.

Crippled by a stroke in 1712, Penn died in Buckinghamshire, England, on July 30, 1718.

For Further Reading

Bronner, Edwin B. *William Penn's "Holy Experiment."* New York: Temple University Publications, 1962.

Dobrée, Bonamy. *William Penn, Quaker and Pioneer.* New York: Houghton Miffin Co., 1932.

Gray, Elizabeth Janet. *Penn.* New York: Viking Press, 1938.

Haviland, Virginia. *William Penn, Founder and Friend.* Nashville, Tenn.: Abingdon-Cokesbury Press, 1952.

Peare, Catherine Owens. *William Penn.* Philadelphia: J. B. Lippincott Co., 1957.

Penn, William. "A Key," Published by the Tract Association of Friends, 1515 Cherry Street, Philadelphia, PA 10102.

Penn, William. "William Penn's Advice to His Children," *Collected Works.* London: J. Sowle, 1726.

Pound, Arthur. *The Penns of Pennsylvania and England.* New York: Macmillian Co., 1932.

Ritchie, Robert C. *Captain Kidd and the War Against the Pirates.* Cambridge, Mass.: Harvard University Press, 1986.